GAMESWARRIOR PRESENTS THE ULTIMATE GUIDE TO POKÉMON

CONTENTS!

4	Welcome!		46-47	Let's Talk About: Rock Types
6	Game Guide: Top 5 Pokémon Core Games		48-49	Let's Talk About: Ghost Types
7	Game Guide: Top 5 Pokémon Remake Games		50-51	Let's Talk About: Dragon Types
8-9	Guide to: Becoming a Pokémon Master		52-53	Let's Talk About: Dark Types
10-11	GamesWarrior Top 5 Starter Pokémon		54-55	Let's Talk About: Steel Types
12-15	All About Types: Every Pokémon Type Explained!		56-57	Let's Talk About: Fairy Types
16-17	Let's Talk About: Water Types		58-59	Let's Talk About: Paradox Pokémon
18-19	Let's Talk About: Fire Types		60	Guide To: Regional Abilities
20-21	Let's Talk About: Grass Types		61	Let's Talk About: Gym Leaders
22-23	Let's Talk About: Normal Types		62	Let's Talk About: Pokémon Trading Card Game
24-25	Let's Talk About: Electric Types		63	Let's Talk About: Pokémon GO
26-27	Let's Talk About: Ice Types		64-65	Game Review: Scarlet and Violet Highlights
28-29	Guide to: Pokéballs		66	Game Guide: Teal Disk
30-31	Let's Talk About: Fighting Types		67	Game Guide: Indigo Disk
32-33	Let's Talk About: Poison Types		68	Anime Guide: Ash Says Goodbye
34-35	Let's Talk About: Ground Types		69	Anime Guide: Ash's Last Movie?
36-37	Let's Talk About: Flying Types		70	Anime Guide: Pokémon Horizons
38-39	Let's Talk About: Psychic Types		71	Anime Guide: Must Watch Series
40-41	Let's Talk About: Bug Types		72-73	Anime Guide: What's Next?
42-43	Let's Talk About: Legendary Pokémon		74-75	Console Review: History of Nintendo and Pokémon
44-45	GamesWarrior Top 5 Mythical Pokémon		76-77	Let's Explore: Pokémon Regions

70 POKÉMON HORIZONS

32-33 POISON TYPES

GAMESWARRIOR

WELCOME!

Welcome to the amazing and unpredictable world of Pokémon! **GamesWarrior** has toured the many regions and trials of the Pokémon world, including meeting all 1025 Pocket Monsters. This isn't any old Annual, this is everything Pokémon trainers need to know, reviewed and translated by your friendly neighbourhood GamesWarrior! **Let's kick things off by going over past and present Pokémon games!**

SCARLET AND VIOLET

In Pokémon Scarlet and Violet, players can explore an open world, meet new friends and set out on exciting quests. The games offer endless possibilities for adventure, with the added ability to explore with friends. The latest Pokémon and stories tie beautifully into the story of the Pokémon world.

★★★★½

GamesWarrior's Verdict: Pokémon Scarlet and Violet are a fresh addition to the Pokémon universe, with their fully open world and unique Terastal phenomenon. The best part is exploring with friends, truly making this the first fully multiplayer Pokémon game.

GamesWarrior's TOP 5 POKÉMON CORE GAMES

GAME GUIDE

Pokémon Scarlet and Violet are the newest games in the main Pokémon series, but did you know there's more than a handful of Pokémon main games? The first games, Pokémon Red and Blue, released back in October 1999, so let's go over the best old school Pokémon core games before Scarlet and Violet.

POKÉMON GOLD AND SILVER

UK Release Date: November 21, 1999
Platform: Game Boy Color

GamesWarrior's Verdict: These games expanded the Pokémon world with the introduction of the Johto region and 100 new Pokémon. The introduction of a real-time day-night cycle and the ability to revisit the Kanto region offered unprecedented depth and replayability. Their ability to connect past and present Pokémon journeys set a new standard for the series.

POKÉMON RED AND BLUE

UK Release Date: February 27, 1996
Platform: Game Boy

GamesWarrior's Verdict: The games that started it all. Pokémon Red and Blue created the foundation for a franchise that has captivated millions worldwide. The concept of catching, battling, and trading Pokémon was revolutionary, offering a mix of strategy, adventure, and collection that has rarely been matched.

POKÉMON X AND Y

UK Release Date: February 12, 2013
Platform: Nintendo 3DS

GamesWarrior's Verdict: These titles brought the Pokémon world into the realm of 3D with stunning graphics and animations. The introduction of the Fairy type and Mega Evolutions breathed new life into the competitive scene, making these games a pivotal point in modernising Pokémon.

POKÉMON RUBY AND SAPPHIRE

UK Release Date: July 23, 2003
Platform: Game Boy Advance

GamesWarrior's Verdict: Introducing the dynamic weather system and having a plot that revolves around natural disasters made Ruby and Sapphire stand out. The lush world of Hoenn and the depth of its lore, along with contests and secret bases, enriched the community and customisation aspects of Pokémon.

POKÉMON BLACK AND WHITE

UK Release Date: March 4, 2011
Platform: Nintendo DS

GamesWarrior's Verdict: These games are celebrated for their strong narrative, which delves into the ethics of Pokémon battles and captures. The introduction of a seasonal cycle, along with vibrant and diverse locations, made Unova a region that feels alive and constantly evolving.

GAMESWARRIOR'S TOP 5 POKÉMON REMAKE GAMES

GAME GUIDE

The Pokémon core series is surrounded by remakes and remasters, often made to tide trainers over until the new adventure releases. Not only is it a great opportunity to revisit a classic Pokémon game, but they're more accessible for those who aren't used to classic Game Boy graphics. Here are our highlights.

POKÉMON FIRERED AND LEAFGREEN

UK Release Date: October 1, 2004
Platform: Game Boy Advance

GW Rating: ★★★★★

GamesWarrior's Verdict: These games bring us back to the Kanto region with brighter colours and even more fun! Pokémon FireRed and LeafGreen are like reading your favourite book but with extra chapters — new islands to explore and more Pokémon to catch. It's a nostalgic journey with fresh surprises!

POKÉMON HEARTGOLD AND SOULSILVER

UK Release Date: March 26, 2010
Platform: Nintendo DS

GW Rating: ★★★★☆

GamesWarrior's Verdict: These games let us revisit the Johto region and have our favourite Pokémon walk alongside us! Pokémon HeartGold and SoulSilver include exciting features like the Pokéathlon, making us feel like proper Pokémon trainers on a grand adventure.

POKÉMON OMEGA RUBY AND ALPHA SAPPHIRE

UK Release Date: November 28, 2014
Platform: Nintendo 3DS

GW Rating: ★★★★½

GamesWarrior's Verdict: These remakes shine with beautiful 3D graphics and introduce the epic Primal Reversion. Omega Ruby and Alpha Sapphire brought back the Hoenn region with more excitement and features, making every storm and sunny day an adventure to remember!

POKÉMON BRILLIANT DIAMOND AND SHINING PEARL

UK Release Date: November 19, 2021
Platform: Nintendo Switch

GW Rating: ★★★★½

GamesWarrior's Verdict: Set in the Sinnoh region with sparkling new visuals and fun gameplay features, Pokémon Brilliant Diamond and Shining Pearl let us dig for treasures, customize bases, and battle in new ways, turning every exploration into a treasure hunt!

POKÉMON LET'S GO, PIKACHU! AND LET'S GO, EEVEE!

UK Release Date: November 16, 2018
Platform: Nintendo Switch

GW Rating: ★★★★☆

GamesWarrior's Verdict: These games reimagine Pokémon Yellow with either Pikachu or Eevee as your partner. The blend of Pokémon GO mechanics with the classic game's journey brings a new twist to stepping out of Pallet Town, making every trip exciting and fresh!

GUIDE TO BECOMING A POKÉMON MASTER

Becoming a Pokémon Master is a big dream for many trainers worldwide, and it's a journey filled with excitement, challenges, and fun! Here's a list of things you can do to step closer to achieving that dream, along with a GamesWarrior verdict on why each step is important.

CATCH LOTS OF POKÉMON

WHAT TO DO: Start by catching as many different Pokémon as possible. Each Pokémon has its unique abilities and strengths.

GamesWarrior's Verdict:
Catching a variety of Pokémon is crucial because it helps you prepare for different challenges. Plus, it's fun to learn about each Pokémon you catch!

TRAIN YOUR POKÉMON

WHAT TO DO: Spend time training your Pokémon to improve their levels and teach them new moves.

GamesWarrior's Verdict:
Training is key to strengthening your Pokémon team. A well-trained Pokémon can make all the difference in battles!

LEARN ABOUT TYPE ADVANTAGES

WHAT TO DO: Understand the strengths and weaknesses of different Pokémon types. For example, water types are strong against fire types but weak against electric.

GamesWarrior's Verdict:
Knowing type advantages can give you a big strategic edge in battles. It's like knowing the secret to winning!

EARN GYM BADGES

WHAT TO DO: Travel from one gym to another and defeat the Gym Leaders to earn badges.

GamesWarrior's Verdict:
Gym badges are proof of your skills and dedication. Collecting them is a major step toward becoming a Pokémon Master!

PARTICIPATE IN TOURNAMENTS

WHAT TO DO: Join Pokémon tournaments to test your skills against other trainers. This could be in video games or the Pokémon TCG.

GamesWarrior's Verdict:
Tournaments are not just about winning but also about learning from others. They're great for gaining experience and confidence.

EXPLORE DIFFERENT REGIONS

WHAT TO DO: Whether in games or through the stories, learning about different Pokémon regions can help you better understand the world of Pokémon.

GamesWarrior's Verdict:
Exploring is important because it opens up new opportunities for encounters and helps you discover more about the Pokémon universe.

TRADE POKÉMON WITH FRIENDS

WHAT TO DO: Trade Pokémon with your friends to catch 'em all. Some Pokémon only evolve through trading!

GamesWarrior's Verdict:
Trading helps you fill your Pokédex and strengthens friendships. Plus, it's the only way to get certain Pokémon!

CARE FOR YOUR POKÉMON

WHAT TO DO: Treat your Pokémon with care and kindness like you would with a pet.

GamesWarrior's Verdict:
Caring for your Pokémon builds a stronger bond, which can be crucial in battles. Pokémon that are treated well perform better!

KEEP LEARNING

WHAT TO DO: Always stay curious and learn new things about the Pokémon world. Read books, watch shows, and talk to more experienced trainers.

GamesWarrior's Verdict:
Knowledge is power! The more you know about Pokémon, the better trainer you'll become.

GAMESWARRIOR'S VERDICT

By following these steps, you'll be on your way to becoming a Pokémon Master. Remember, the journey is just as important as the goal, so have fun and keep pushing forward, young trainers!

TOP 5 GAMES WARRIOR'S STARTER

TYPE: FIRE
CHARMANDER

This little fire lizard, can evolve into the fierce and fiery Charizard, who can fly and breathe fire! It is a hot favourite for many trainers looking to start their journey with a spark!

GW RATING ★★★★★

THIS POKÉMON IS SUPER COOL AND BRAVE.

TYPE: GRASS/POISON
BULBASAUR

This Pokémon carries a seed on its back that grows into a big plant as it evolves. It's chosen by trainers who want a steady and reliable friend to explore the world.

GW RATING ★★★★½

BULBASAUR IS AS STURDY AS THEY COME!

TYPE: WATER
SQUIRTLE

The tiny turtle Squirtle can accurately spray water from its mouth. This cool water Pokémon can evolve into Blastoise, with powerful water cannons on its shell!

GW RATING ★★★★½

SQUIRTLE IS A BLAST FOR ANYONE WHO WANTS TO MAKE A SPLASH!

POKÉMON

Players can start their adventures with some of the coolest and most lovable Pokémon. GamesWarrior has scoured the Pokémon world to bring you the best top 5 starter Pokémon ever!

TYPE: ELECTRIC
PIKACHU

Pikachu is probably the most famous Pokémon, and for good reason! It's a sparkling companion on the roads of Pokémon training and always ready to charge up the atmosphere!

GW RATING ★★★★☆

ELECTRIFYINGLY CUTE WITH ELECTRICITY ZAPPING CHEEKS!

TYPE: WATER
MUDKIP

Mudkip, the water fish Pokémon, can sense air and water current changes with its fin. This makes it a clever and intuitive pick for any trainer.

GW RATING ★★★★☆

WHO CAN RESIST THAT CUTE FACE AND POWER?

GAMESWARRIOR'S VERDICT

GamesWarrior believes that these starters bring a lot of personality to your Pokémon team and offer strengths that can help any trainer become a Pokémon Master. Each Pokémon has unique abilities and fantastic evolutions that make them stars from the start of your adventure!

ALL ABOUT TYPES

EVERY POKÉMON TYPE EXPLAINED!

GAMESWARRIOR has captured all the information trainers need to know about Pokémon types. Use this breakdown to get the **STRENGTHS** and **WEAKNESS** details you need on the (Pokémon) go!

BUG

STRONG AGAINST
Dark, Grass and Psychic

WEAK AGAINST
Fire, Flying and Rock

Bug-type Pokémon are strong early on but become weak later. They're effective against Grass, Psychic, and Dark-type Pokémon. Some, like Scizor and Volcarona, are powerful in high-level play. Quick evolution gives an early advantage, but they have common weaknesses and lower stats.

GW RATING ★★★☆☆
FOR STARTER TEAMS

SCIZOR | VOLCARONA

DARK

STRONG AGAINST
Ghost and Psychic

WEAK AGAINST
Bug, Fairy and Fighting

Dark-type Pokémon excel at surprise attacks, are immune to Psychic-type moves, and are effective against Psychic and Ghost types. They are valuable in battles, but their weaknesses require careful play.

GW RATING ★★★☆☆
FOR TAKING DOWN SPOOKY POKÉMON

UMBREON | TYRANITAR

DRAGON

STRONG AGAINST
Dragon

WEAK AGAINST
Dragon, Fairy and Ice

Dragon-type Pokémon are strong against other Dragons but weak against Ice, Dragon, and Fairy types. They're great for skilled trainers.

GW RATING ★★★★☆
FOR POWERFUL MOVES

GARCHOMP | MEGA CHARIZARD X

ELECTRIC

STRONG AGAINST
Flying and Water

WEAK AGAINST
Ground

Electric-type Pokémon are known for their high-speed stats and powerful Electric-type moves that make them resilient against various opponents. They have an advantage against many opponents but are vulnerable to ground-type attacks.

GW RATING ★★★★☆
FOR SPEED

PICHU | THUNDURUS

FAIRY

STRONG AGAINST
Dark, Dragon and Fighting

WEAK AGAINST
Poison and Steel

Fairy-type Pokémon have mystical abilities, are strong against Dragon, Dark, and Fighting types, but weak against Steel and Poison types. They offer a balance of offense and defense when used properly.

GW RATING ★★★★☆
FOR TYPE COVERAGE

GALARIAN RAPIDASH | AZUMARILL

FIGHTING

STRONG AGAINST
Dark, Ice, Normal, Rock and Steel

WEAK AGAINST
Fairy, Flying and Psychic

Fighting-type Pokémon excel in close combat and offer unmatched physical strength. They are powerful warriors and can turn the tide of battle.

GW RATING ★★★★★
FOR THEIR STRENGTH

HITMONLEE | HITMONCHAN

FIRE

STRONG AGAINST
Bug, Grass and Steel
WEAK AGAINST
Ground, Rock and Water

Fire-type Pokémon are powerful in battle, good against Grass, Ice, Bug, and Steel, but weak against Water, Rock, and Ground. They symbolise warmth, light, and destruction.

GW Rating: ★★★★☆
FOR TAKING DOWN STEEL TYPES

GMAX CHARIZARD — INCINEROAR

FLYING

STRONG AGAINST
Bug, Fighting and Grass
WEAK AGAINST
Electric, Ice and Rock

Flying-type Pokémon are aerial masters and strong against Grass, Fighting, and Bug types, but weak against Electric, Ice, and Rock-type moves.

GW Rating: ★★★★☆
FOR TAKING DOWN BUG TYPES

GYRADOS — SHINY HISUIAN BRAVIARY

GHOST

STRONG AGAINST
Ghost and Psychic
WEAK AGAINST
Dark and Ghost

Ghost-type Pokémon are immune to Normal and Fighting moves. They manipulate the battlefield and are unpredictable, with Gengar and Mimikyu being prime examples.

GW Rating: ★★★★☆
FOR TURNING BATTLES AROUND

MEGA GENGAR — CERULEDGE

NORMAL

STRONG AGAINST
None
WEAK AGAINST
Fighting

Normal-type Pokémon are versatile, balanced, and unpredictable. Examples include Snorlax and Blissey, and they make a solid foundation for a capable team.

GW Rating: ★★★☆☆
FOR OUTLASTING OPPONENTS

CHANSEY — KANGASKHAN

POISON

STRONG AGAINST
Fairy and Grass
WEAK AGAINST
Ground and Psychic

Poison Pokémon wear down foes with toxins, control the battlefield, and excel at attrition warfare. They're strong against Grass/Fairy types and weak against Ground/Psychic moves. They're valuable for endurance-focused trainers.

GW Rating: ★★★★★
FOR POISONOUS STATUS EFFECTS

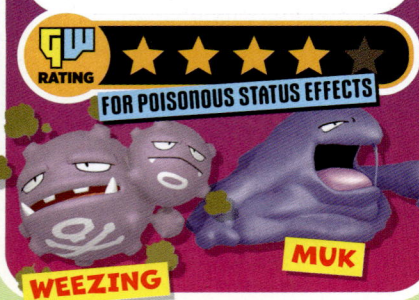
WEEZING — MUK

PSYCHIC

STRONG AGAINST
Fighting and Poison
WEAK AGAINST
Bug, Dark and Ghost

Psychic-type Pokémon use mental abilities, predict battles, and excel against Fighting and Poison types. Examples include Alakazam and Espeon. They offer a strategic path to victory.

GW Rating: ★★★★☆
FOR SPECIAL MOVES

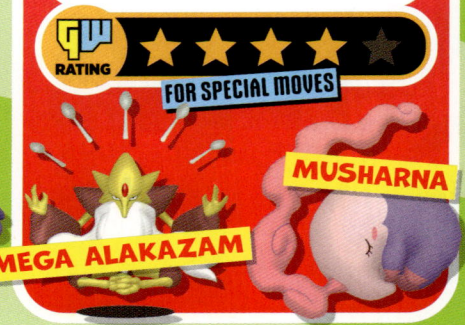
MEGA ALAKAZAM — MUSHARNA

GRASS

STRONG AGAINST
Dark, Grass and Psychic

WEAK AGAINST
Fire, Flying and Rock

Grass-type Pokémon embody nature and excel against some types while facing challenges from others. They are essential to any team, bringing life and endurance to battles.

GW RATING ★★★★☆
FOR STATUS EFFECTS

MOW ROTOM • GOGOAT

GROUND

STRONG AGAINST
Electric, Fire, Poison, Rock and Steel

WEAK AGAINST
Grass, Ice and Water

Ground-type Pokémon are powerful, versatile, and deeply connected to the earth. Despite their elemental challenges, they offer natural strength and strategic depth that can turn the tides of battle.

GW RATING ★★★★☆
FOR TYPE COVERAGE

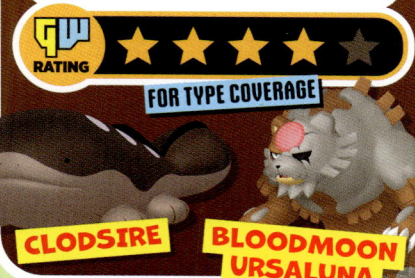

CLODSIRE • BLOODMOON URSALUNA

ICE

STRONG AGAINST
Dragon, Flying and Grass

WEAK AGAINST
Fighting, Fire, Rock and Steel

Ice-type Pokémon have freezing abilities, are strong against certain types, weak against others, and can control the battlefield with frost and snow. Articuno and Lapras are among the most potent Ice-type Pokémon.

GW RATING ★★★☆☆
FOR TAKING DOWN DRAGON TYPES

EISCUE • FROSMOTH

ROCK

STRONG AGAINST
Bug, Fire, Flying and Ice

WEAK AGAINST
Fighting, Grass, Ground, Steel and Water

Rock-type Pokémon are strong and powerful, with moves like Stone Edge and Rock Slide. They can absorb hits and strike back with earth-shattering force, making them foundational to any team.

GW RATING ★★★☆☆
FOR TAKING DOWN FIRE TYPES QUICKLY

KLEAVOR • GIGALITH

STEEL

STRONG AGAINST
Fairy, Ice and Rock

WEAK AGAINST
Fighting, Fire and Ground

Steel-type Pokémon are tough and resistant, with powerful attacks. They're vulnerable to certain moves, but their overall versatility makes them essential in battles.

GW RATING ★★★★★
FOR TAKING DOWN POWERFUL FAIRY TYPES

STEELIX • CORVIKNIGHT

WATER

STRONG AGAINST
Fire, Ground and Rock

WEAK AGAINST
Electric and Grass

Water-type Pokémon are vital and adaptable, strong against Fire, Ground, and Rock types, but weak against Electric and Grass types.

GW RATING ★★★★☆
FOR WASHING AWAY POPULAR TYPINGS

WALKING WAKE • POLIWRATH

LET'S TALK ABOUT... WATER TYPES

WATER TYPES are the versatile and resilient Pokémon of the aquatic world, adapting fluidly to many battle scenarios! They wield moves like **Hydro Pump** and **Surf** that harness the power of water to overwhelm opponents with both force and finesse. Water types are particularly effective against Fire, Ground, and Rock types, showcasing their ability to extinguish and erode with ease. Electric and Grass types can be a problem, which can disrupt their flow and absorb their strength. Pokémon like **Gyarados** and **Blastoise** are like the tidal forces of Water Pokémon because they combine immense power with strategic depth.

LET'S DIVE INTO WHICH MOVES AND WATER POKÉMON GAMESWARRIOR THINKS ARE THE MOST IMPACTFUL!

WATER MOVES

HYDRO PUMP

WHAT IT DOES: Fires a high-pressure stream of water at the target, one of the strongest Water-type moves.

GamesWarrior's Verdict: This move is a powerhouse, perfect for delivering a crushing blow with the sheer force of water!

SURF

WHAT IT DOES: Creates a wave that crashes over the battlefield, hitting all adjacent Pokémon.

GamesWarrior's Verdict: It's excellent for battles involving multiple opponents, showing that Water types can control the arena with their wave-making capabilities.

AQUA TAIL

WHAT IT DOES: The user attacks by swinging its tail like a vicious wave in a raging sea.

GamesWarrior's Verdict: This move combines physical prowess with the natural power of water, making it both versatile and potent.

WHIRLPOOL

WHAT IT DOES: Traps the opponent in a swirling vortex, inflicting damage for four to five turns.

GamesWarrior's Verdict: It's a strategic move that not only damages but also restricts the opponent, showcasing the controlling nature of Water types.

RAIN DANCE

WHAT IT DOES: Summons rain to boost Water-type moves for five turns.

GamesWarrior's Verdict: This move sets the stage for enhanced Water-type tactics, turning the weather into a strategic ally.

WATER POKÉMON

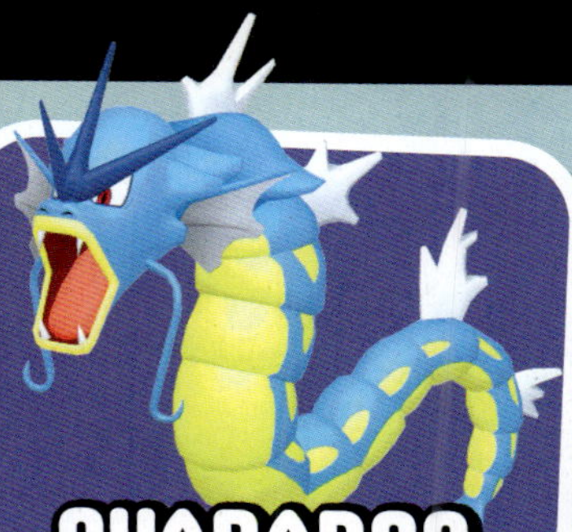

GYARADOS

ALL ABOUT: Gyarados rises from the serene Magikarp with a ferocious temperament and overwhelming power.

STRENGTHS: Known for its destructive capabilities and intimidating presence.

GamesWarrior's Verdict: Gyarados is a symbol of transformation and raw power, making it a fearsome and respected figure in any battle.

GW RATING ★★★★★

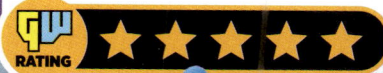

BLASTOISE

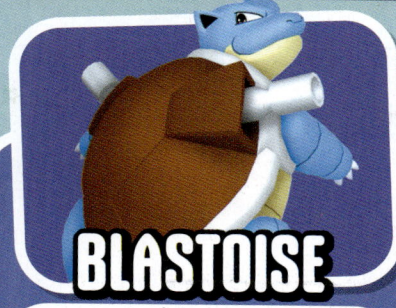

ALL ABOUT: Blastoise can accurately shoot torrents of water from the hydro cannons on its back.

STRENGTHS: Its shell provides formidable defence, and its cannons allow long-range assaults.

GamesWarrior's Verdict: Blastoise is like a mobile fortress, capable of launching powerful water strikes with pinpoint accuracy.

GW RATING ★★★★☆

VAPOREAN

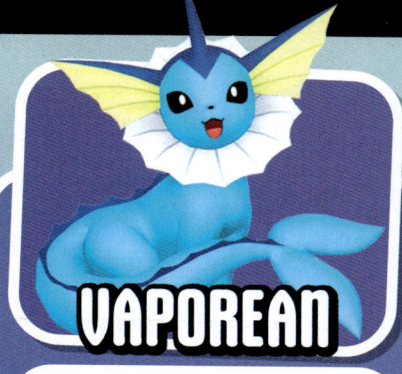

ALL ABOUT: Vaporeon can dissolve into water, making it nearly invisible in aquatic environments.

STRENGTHS: It is highly adaptable and can recover health quickly in water.

GamesWarrior's Verdict: Vaporeon represents the adaptive and elusive nature of Water types, using its environment to heal and hide.

GW RATING ★★★★☆

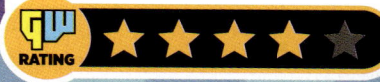

LAPRAS

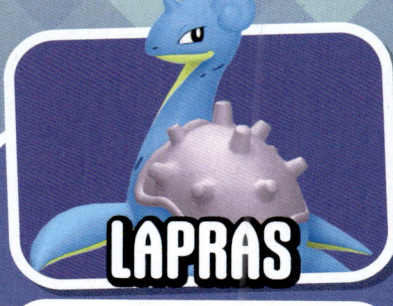

ALL ABOUT: Lapras is gentle but can ferry people across bodies of water, using its singing to soothe and its ice moves to protect.

STRENGTHS: Combines water and ice techniques to provide versatile combat options.

GamesWarrior's Verdict: Lapras is both a guardian and a gentle giant, offering safe passage and protective ice barriers in tumultuous waters.

GW RATING ★★★★☆

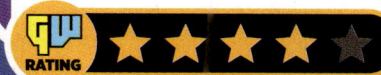

MILOTIC

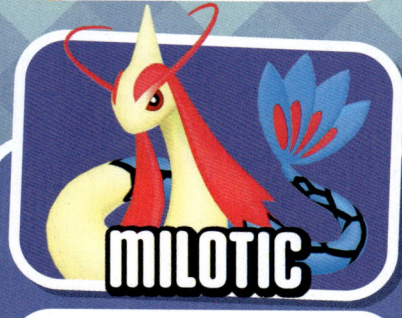

ALL ABOUT: Milotic is renowned for its beauty and calming aura, which can quell anger and hostility.

STRENGTHS: It's incredibly resilient and can restore its health automatically under the right conditions.

GamesWarrior's Verdict: Milotic brings a blend of elegance and endurance to battles, representing the serene yet powerful nature of Water types.

GW RATING ★★★☆☆

?

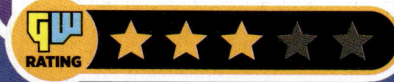

WHO'S YOUR FAVOURITE WATER POKÉMON? MAYBE THE MIGHTY GYARADOS OR THE STRATEGIC BLASTOISE? WATER POKÉMON SURELY KNOW HOW TO MAKE WAVES IN ANY FIGHT!

What GAMESWARRIOR loves most!

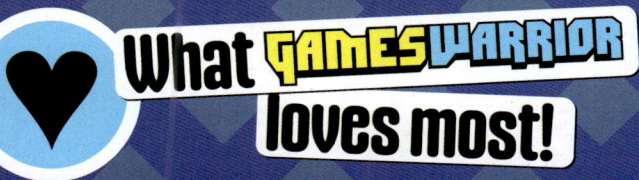

Water Pokémon are the essence of adaptability and strength, able to shape the battle environment to their advantage! GameWarrior's favourite is Gyarados for its dramatic evolution from vulnerability to a titanic force, embodying the unpredictable power of Water types.

LET'S TALK ABOUT...
FIRE TYPES

FIRE TYPES are the blazing stars of the Pokémon world, lighting up battles with fiery moves! They have hot moves like **Flamethrower** and **Fire Blast** that can burn through the competition. Fire types are fantastic at scorching Grass, Bug, Ice, and Steel types, showing their power to melt and consume. But they have to be careful around Water, Rock, and Ground types, which can smother their flames. Pokémon like **Charizard** and **Arcanine** are like the torchbearers of Fire Pokémon because they're so powerful and inspiring.

LET'S DISCOVER WHICH MOVES AND FIRE POKÉMON GAMESWARRIOR THINKS ARE THE HOTTEST!

FIRE MOVES

FLAMETHROWER
WHAT IT DOES: Shoots a stream of fire that can also leave the opponent burned.

GamesWarrior's Verdict: This move is awesome because it's like wielding a fire hose that's too hot to handle!

FIRE BLAST
WHAT IT DOES: Unleashes a massive burst of fire in a shape that can scare and singe foes.

GamesWarrior's Verdict: It's like dropping a firebomb on the battlefield, showing the explosive power of Fire types!

HEAT WAVE
WHAT IT DOES: Sends a wave of intense heat that can hit multiple opponents at once.

GamesWarrior's Verdict: This move is great for taking on several foes, like turning up the summer heat to the max!

INFERNO
WHAT IT DOES: Engulfs the opponent in flames with a high chance of leaving them burned.

GamesWarrior's Verdict: It's like setting off a wildfire in the battle, tough for any opponent to handle!

LAVA PLUME
WHAT IT DOES: Erupts and covers the battlefield in flames, hitting everyone nearby and possibly burning them.

GamesWarrior's Verdict: This move is like a volcano erupting right in the middle of the fight, spreading fire everywhere!

FIRE POKÉMON

CHARIZARD

ALL ABOUT: Charizard flies through the sky and can breathe fire hot enough to melt boulders.

STRENGTHS: Known for its ability to fly and its fiery breath, which makes it a fearsome sight in the sky.

GamesWarrior's Verdict: Charizard is like a dragon of legend, capable of ruling the skies and scorching the earth below.

ARCANINE

ALL ABOUT: Arcanine is majestic and fast, known as the Legendary Pokémon for its swift movements and noble appearance.

STRENGTHS: It's incredibly fast and emits a comforting heat, making it a warm companion.

GamesWarrior's Verdict: Arcanine is amazing for its speed and proud appearance, making it both a loyal friend and a formidable foe.

NINETALES

ALL ABOUT: Ninetales is a beautiful Pokémon with nine tails, each holding mystical powers.

STRENGTHS: Known for its intelligence and the curse-inducing powers of its tails.

GamesWarrior's Verdict: Ninetales is enchanting with its mystical aura and the legends surrounding its existence.

BLAZIKEN

ALL ABOUT: Blaziken can kick with flames that cover its legs, making its martial arts fiery and fierce.

STRENGTHS: Combines physical power with the heat of fire in its fighting techniques.

GamesWarrior's Verdict: Blaziken is like a fiery fighter, using its powerful legs to deliver explosive, burning kicks.

RAPIDASH

ALL ABOUT: Rapidash gallops at incredible speeds, leaving fire trails behind it.

STRENGTHS: Its speed is unmatched, and it can run so fast that it looks like it's flying.

GamesWarrior's Verdict: Rapidash is like a shooting star on land, blazing across the battlefield with unmatched grace and speed.

MAGMAR

ALL ABOUT: Magmar controls fire and can spit fiery blasts from its mouth to incinerate everything around it.

STRENGTHS: It thrives in volcanic regions and uses its fiery powers to maintain its territory.

GamesWarrior's Verdict: Magmar is like the guardian of flames, using its control over fire to challenge any opponent.

Fire Pokémon bring warmth and light to every battle with bold and bright flames! GamesWarrior's absolute favourite is Blaziken because it combines fiery passion with martial prowess in a spectacular display of power.

LET'S TALK ABOUT...
GRASS TYPES

GRASS TYPES are the nature-loving Pokémon that thrive with the power of the earth beneath their roots! They wield leafy moves like Leaf Blade and Solar Beam that harness the energy of nature to outgrow their competition. Grass types are superb at taking down Water, Ground, and Rock types, demonstrating their ability to sprout against the odds. However, they must be cautious around Fire, Ice, Poison, Flying, and Bug types, which can trim their leaves quickly. Pokémon like Venusaur and Breloom are like the guardians of the forest among Grass Pokémon because they're so robust and nurturing.

LET'S DISCOVER WHICH MOVES AND GRASS POKÉMON GAMESWARRIOR THINKS ARE THE GREENEST!

GRASS MOVES

LEAF BLADE
WHAT IT DOES: Slashes the opponent with a sharp leaf, often landing a critical hit.

GamesWarrior's Verdict: This move is sharp and swift, cutting through the competition like a hot knife through butter!

★★★★☆

SOLAR BEAM
WHAT IT DOES: Absorbs sunlight on the first turn and releases it as a powerful beam on the second turn.

GamesWarrior's Verdict: It's like charging up all the power of the sun to unleash a devastating blast of energy!

★★★★★

GIGA DRAIN
WHAT IT DOES: Absorbs health from the opponent, transferring it back to the user.

GamesWarrior's Verdict: This move is great because it saps strength from foes and revitalises the user, showing the resilient cycle of nature!

★★★★☆

SPORE
WHAT IT DOES: Releases spores that put the opponent to sleep.

GamesWarrior's Verdict: It's like using nature's lullaby to gently put opponents to sleep, giving a strategic advantage.

★★★★☆

POWER WHIP
WHAT IT DOES: Lashes out with a vigorous vine whip that deals heavy damage.

GamesWarrior's Verdict: This move packs a powerful punch with the strength of a hundred vines, making it incredibly forceful and effective.

★★★★☆

GRASS POKÉMON

VENUSAUR

ALL ABOUT: Venusaur harnesses the power of sunlight to grow and strengthen its formidable floral features.

STRENGTHS: Known for its large flower that can absorb sunlight and use it to power up its moves.

GamesWarrior's Verdict: Venusaur is like a mobile forest, bringing life and energy wherever it goes, making it a powerhouse in battles.

BRELOOM

ALL ABOUT: Breloom can stretch its arms to deliver speedy punches, releasing spores from the holes in its cap.

STRENGTHS: It combines the force of Fighting techniques with the cunning of Grass tactics.

GamesWarrior's Verdict: Breloom is unique as it blends the agility of a fighter with the subtlety of a naturalist, making it a versatile and surprising contender.

SCEPTILE

ALL ABOUT: Sceptile is swift and agile, darting through the forest quickly and attacking with razor-sharp leaves.

STRENGTHS: Known for its speed and the cutting leaves that grow back instantly even if they fall.

GamesWarrior's Verdict: Sceptile is like the ninja of the forest, quick and deadly with a strike that's as fast as it is silent.

TORTERRA

ALL ABOUT: Torterra carries an entire ecosystem on its back, complete with a large tree and various other plants.

STRENGTHS: Its size and strength make it a formidable barrier, connecting deeply with the earth.

GamesWarrior's Verdict: Torterra is like a walking nature preserve, embodying the enduring strength and stability of the Earth itself.

ROSELIA

ALL ABOUT: Roselia emits beautiful floral scents and can strike with thorny attacks.

STRENGTHS: Its aroma can soothe friends and repel foes, while its thorns ensure it isn't underestimated.

GamesWarrior's Verdict: Roselia combines beauty and danger, making it both enchanting and formidable in defence.

LEAFEON

ALL ABOUT: Leafeon undergoes photosynthesis with its leafy tail, staying energetically charged.

STRENGTHS: It's exceptionally efficient at using sunlight to power its botanical abilities.

GamesWarrior's Verdict: Leafeon is like the solar panel of Pokémon, using sunlight to stay active and alert while battling with graceful moves.

Grass Pokémon are not just about battling; they bring a touch of nature's wonder to every fight! GamesWarrior's absolute favourite is Venusaur for its ability to embody the power and nurturing essence of the forest.

LET'S TALK ABOUT... NORMAL TYPES

NORMAL TYPES are the versatile all-rounders of the Pokémon world, adept at adapting to a wide range of battle scenarios! They wield a diverse array of moves like Hyper Beam and Body Slam that rely on sheer power and cunning tactics. Normal types aren't super effective against any specific type. Still, they can hit most types without resistance, except for Ghost types, which are immune. However, they must watch out for Fighting types, which can deliver a heavy blow to them. Pokémon like Snorlax and Blissey are like the foundation of Normal Pokémon because they combine incredible resilience with potent capabilities.

LET'S DIVE INTO WHICH MOVES AND NORMAL POKÉMON GAMESWARRIOR THINKS ARE THE MOST RESOURCEFUL!

NORMAL MOVES

HYPER BEAM
WHAT IT DOES: Unleashes a massive burst of energy that requires recharging the next turn.

GamesWarrior's Verdict: This move is like pulling out all the stops for a show-stopping power play that can turn the tide of any battle!

★★★★★

BODY SLAM
WHAT IT DOES: The user slams into the opponent, possibly causing paralysis.

GamesWarrior's Verdict: It's great for not just dealing damage but also potentially immobilising your opponent, adding a strategic twist.

★★★★☆

DOUBLE-EDGE
WHAT IT DOES: A reckless, all-out charge that also recoils some damage back to the user.

GamesWarrior's Verdict: This move is a testament to bravery, risking harm for potential great reward.

★★★★☆

SING
WHAT IT DOES: A soothing melody that lulls the opponent to sleep.

GamesWarrior's Verdict: It's a clever tactic to disable opponents, showcasing that battles aren't always about brute force.

★★★★☆

QUICK ATTACK
WHAT IT DOES: Strikes first with a swift attack.

GamesWarrior's Verdict: Perfect for getting the upper hand early in a battle, proving that speed can be as crucial as strength.

★★★★☆

NORMAL POKÉMON

SNORLAX

ALL ABOUT: Snorlax blocks paths with its massive body when asleep. It's almost impossible to move.

STRENGTHS: Known for its incredible durability and dishing out significant damage.

GamesWarrior's Verdict: Snorlax is like a boulder that can withstand and deliver powerful blows, embodying resilience and strength.

BLISSEY

ALL ABOUT: Blissey can heal wounds with its egg, which it shares with those who are hurt.

STRENGTHS: Renowned for its extraordinary healing powers and vast health pool.

GamesWarrior's Verdict: Blissey symbolises kindness and durability, making it a cornerstone of any defensive strategy.

PORYGON-2

ALL ABOUT: Porygon-2 is a virtual creature capable of converting into data to enter cyberspace.

STRENGTHS: It's highly adaptable and can perform various types of attacks.

GamesWarrior's Verdict: Porygon-2 is a testament to innovation, using its digital prowess to outmanoeuvre physical and special opponents alike.

URSARING

ALL ABOUT: Ursaring searches for honey with its keen sense of smell, becoming a fearsome foe when angry.

STRENGTHS: Its physical prowess is formidable, capable of overpowering many adversaries.

GamesWarrior's Verdict: Combining raw power with a ferocious nature, Ursaring is a fierce physical Pokémon.

STARAPTOR

ALL ABOUT: Staraptor soars the skies, fearlessly attacking its enemies with powerful aerial moves.

STRENGTHS: Combines speed and power to execute devastating strikes.

GamesWarrior's Verdict: Staraptor showcases the aggressive side of Normal types, striking hard and fast from above.

?

WHO'S YOUR FAVOURITE NORMAL POKÉMON? MAYBE THE STURDY SNORLAX OR THE CARING BLISSEY? NORMAL POKÉMON SURELY KNOW HOW TO MAKE THEIR PRESENCE FELT!

What GAMESWARRIOR loves most!

Normal Pokémon are proof that sometimes, being versatile and robust is the best strategy in battles! GamesWarrior's favourite is Snorlax for its unmatched staying power and the sheer impact it can make in fights.

LET'S TALK ABOUT... ELECTRIC TYPES

ELECTRIC TYPES are the sparky and energetic Pokémon that light up the battle! They have zippy moves like Thunderbolt and Volt Switch that can shock and awe their opponents. Electric types are fantastic at zapping Water and Flying types. Still, it would help if you watched for Ground types immune to electric shocks. Pokémon like Pikachu and Jolteon are like the live wires of Electric Pokémon because they're so fast and powerful.

LET'S SEE WHAT MOVES AND ELECTRIC POKÉMON GAMESWARRIOR THINKS ARE THE BRIGHTEST!

ELECTRIC MOVES

THUNDERBOLT

WHAT IT DOES: A strong electric blast that can sometimes make the opponent unable to move.

GamesWarrior's Verdict: This move is electrifying because it packs a powerful punch and can stop others in their tracks!

 ★★★★☆

VOLT SWITCH

WHAT IT DOES: Hits the opponent, then lets you switch with another Pokémon, keeping the battle in your favour.

GamesWarrior's Verdict: It's like hitting and running, which is a smart way to stay ahead of the game!

 ★★★★★

THUNDER WAVE

WHAT IT DOES: A jolt that doesn't hurt much but can paralyse the opponent, making them slower or stopping them from moving.

GamesWarrior's Verdict: It's sneaky because it slows down the other Pokémon, giving you a big advantage!

  ★★★★☆

WILD CHARGE

WHAT IT DOES: It is a risky, strong move that also hurts the user a little.

GamesWarrior's Verdict: This move is like going all out with a big boom, showing you're brave and ready to win!

 ★★★☆☆

ELECTRO BALL

WHAT IT DOES: The faster your Pokémon is compared to the other, the more damage this move does.

GamesWarrior's Verdict: It's awesome because the quicker you are, the stronger you hit, making speed super important!

 ★★★★☆

ELECTRIC POKÉMON

PIKACHU

ALL ABOUT: Pikachu is the most famous Electric Pokémon. It can zap with electricity and is super cute.

STRENGTHS: Pikachu can quickly learn various electric moves to zap opponents.

GamesWarrior's Verdict: Pikachu is amazing in battles because it's adorable and can also deliver a powerful shock.

JOLTEON

ALL ABOUT: Jolteon is like a lightning bolt on legs; it is super fast and can shock with powerful electricity.

STRENGTHS: It's one of the quickest Pokémon, and its attacks can pack a punch.

GamesWarrior's Verdict: Jolteon is incredible because its speed and shock power makes it a tough opponet.

LUXRAY

ALL ABOUT: Luxray looks like a cool electric lion that can see through walls and zap with strong electric attacks.

STRENGTHS: It's powerful and has a majestic presence, making it a fearless leader in battles.

GamesWarrior's Verdict: Luxray is like the king of electric Pokémon because it's strong, brave, and can lead the way.

ELECTIVIRE

ALL ABOUT: Electivire has plug-like tails that can deliver powerful electric shocks to anything it touches.

STRENGTHS: It's really strong, and its electric shocks can power up its punches.

GamesWarrior's Verdict: Electivire is cool because it's like a powerhouse, ready to electrify the competition.

RAICHU

ALL ABOUT: Raichu is the evolved form of Pikachu and can deliver even bigger electric shocks.

STRENGTHS: It's a bit bigger and stronger than Pikachu, making its electric attacks even more powerful.

GamesWarrior's Verdict: Raichu is great because it shows how growing up can make you even stronger and cooler.

ZAPDOS

ALL ABOUT: Zapdos is a legendary bird that controls electricity and can summon thunderstorms.

STRENGTHS: It's incredibly powerful, can fly, and has legendary electric shocks.

GamesWarrior's Verdict: Zapdos is awe-inspiring because it's like the master of thunder and lightning, ruling the skies.

What GAMESWARRIOR loves most! Electric Pokémon are full of energy and always ready to light up any battle with their shocking moves! GamesWarrior's all-time favourite is Pikachu because it's not only powerful but also brings a spark of joy to any battle.

LET'S TALK ABOUT... ICE TYPES

ICE TYPES are the chilling champions of the Pokémon world, mastering the frosty elements to cool the heat of battle! They wield freezing moves like Ice Beam and Blizzard that can stop opponents cold in their tracks. Ice types are fantastic at dealing with Dragon, Grass, Flying, and Ground types, showing their ability to take advantage of their frosty powers. They need to watch out for Fire, Fighting, Rock, and Steel types, which can melt or shatter their icy form. Pokémon like Articuno and Glaceon are like the glacial guardians of Ice Pokémon because they can command the cold with elegance and power.

LET'S EXPLORE WHICH MOVES AND ICE POKÉMON GAMESWARRIOR THINKS ARE THE COOLEST!

ICE MOVES

ICE BEAM

WHAT IT DOES: Shoots a beam of ice that may freeze the target.

GamesWarrior's Verdict: A brilliant move, combining power with the chance to stop foes dead in their tracks by freezing!

★★★★★

BLIZZARD

WHAT IT DOES: Unleashes a fierce snowstorm that hits all opponents and has a higher chance of freezing them.

GamesWarrior's Verdict: It's like unleashing a winter storm in the middle of battle, overwhelming with its sheer intensity!

★★★★☆

AVALANCHE

WHAT IT DOES: Strikes back with double the power if the user has been hurt by the opponent in the same turn.

GamesWarrior's Verdict: A great move for turning the tide, using the opponent's aggression against them like a true winter warrior!

★★★★☆

FROST BREATH

WHAT IT DOES: Always results in a critical hit, showing it's cold but precise in striking.

GamesWarrior's Verdict: It's like a sudden winter gust that's sharp and always hits where it hurts the most.

★★★★☆

ICE SHARD

WHAT IT DOES: A quick ice attack that always hits first.

GamesWarrior's Verdict: This move is like a swift icicle thrown at the start of a confrontation, quick and chillingly effective!

★★★★☆

ICE POKÉMON

ARTICUNO

ALL ABOUT: Articuno rules the skies with its icy wings, causing snow to fall as it flies.

STRENGTHS: Known for its majestic and serene presence, it can chill the air just by being nearby.

GameWarrior Verdict: Articuno is like the monarch of winter skies, both beautiful and formidable with its frosty dominion.

GLACEON

ALL ABOUT: Glaceon can freeze its fur to make icicles, turning its body into a frosty weapon.

STRENGTHS: It controls its body temperature to freeze the surrounding air and create icy attacks.

GameWarrior Verdict: Glaceon is amazing because it embodies the essence of ice, using its cold beauty as a powerful defence and offence.

WALREIN

ALL ABOUT: Walrein uses its large body and tusks to break ice and defend against foes.

STRENGTHS: Its bulk makes it resilient in battle and it can endure harsh cold like no other.

GameWarrior Verdict: Walrein is like a frosty tank, tough and unyielding in the frozen battlegrounds it thrives in.

MAMOSWINE

ALL ABOUT: Mamoswine ploughs through ice and snow with its massive tusks, a true behemoth of the tundra.

STRENGTHS: Its size and strength allow it to endure and charge through even the toughest conditions.

GamesWarrior's Verdict: Mamoswine is a powerhouse of the ice world, unstoppable in its charge and enduring against all odds.

AURORUS

ALL ABOUT: Surviving since prehistoric times, Aurorus can create ice walls and unleash freezing blasts.

STRENGTHS: It uniquely affects the weather, bringing a chill that benefits its icy tactics.

GamesWarrior's Verdict: Aurorus is like a living relic of ancient times, majestic and powerful with its ability to control the cold.

FROSLASS

ALL ABOUT: Froslass, the snowy ghost, freezes foes with a chilling gaze and is known for its haunting beauty.

STRENGTHS: It combines Ice and Ghost tactics to slip past defences and freeze opponents with eerie precision.

GamesWarrior's Verdict: Froslass is captivating with its spectral chill, blending beauty and fear in a haunting dance of ice.

What **GAMESWARRIOR** loves most!

Ice Pokémon bring a touch of winter's majesty to every battle, chilling the hearts of their foes while dazzling spectators with their crystalline manoeuvres! GamesWarrior's favourite is Articuno for its regal presence and commanding control over the icy elements.

GUIDE TO POKÉBALLS!

Pokéballs are essential for trainers to carry with them at all times. They are devices used to catch and store Pokémon, taking advantage of a Pokémon's ability to shrink to any size. **Let's explore some of the best Pokéballs you can use on your adventure!**

GamesWarrior TOP 5 POKEBALLS

ULTRA BALL

The Ultra Ball is like the superhero of Pokéballs! It has a much higher chance of catching Pokémon than most other balls. It's both powerful and reliable — a must-have for every Pokémon trainer!

  ★★★★★

If you're trying to catch a Pokémon that's really hard to get, the Ultra Ball is your best friend.

MASTER BALL

The rare Master Ball is the stuff of legends! It can catch any Pokémon without fail. Yep, you heard that right — any Pokémon at all!

 ★★★★★

Save it for a particular Pokémon you must catch.

QUICK BALL

Quick Ball is perfect for those fast moments at the start of a battle. It works best if used when you encounter a Pokémon. The quicker you throw it, the better your chances.

 ★★★★½

It's like catching Pokémon at lightning speed!

LUXURY BALL

The Luxury Ball is about pampering your Pokémon and it will make them happy in no time! Any Pokémon caught with this ball becomes friendlier towards you faster than usual.

 ★★★★½

It's like giving your new Pokémon pal a first-class home!

DIVE BALL

Dive into the blue with this amazing Pokéball!! It works best when catching Pokémon that live in water or when fishing. It's like having a special key to unlock the watery world of Pokémon.

 ★★★★☆

Dive Ball is the dream for anyone who loves water adventures!

GamesWarrior's VERDICT

GamesWarrior hopes this helps pick the perfect Pokéball for your adventure. Each of these balls has a unique flair and special use, making your Pokémon journey even more fun and exciting! Remember, the right Pokéball can make all the difference in catching your favourite Pokémon.

LET'S TALK ABOUT... FIGHTING TYPES

FIGHTING TYPES are the tough and brave Pokémon who love to get up close and personal in battles! They have powerful moves like **Close Combat** and **Dynamic Punch** that show off their incredible strength and fighting spirit. Fighting types are fantastic against Normal, Ice, Rock, and Steel types, showcasing their ability to break through defences. However, they need to watch out for Flying, Psychic, and Fairy types, which can give them a tough match. Pokémon like **Machamp** and **Lucario** are like the champions of Fighting Pokémon because they're so strong and skilled.

LET'S FIND OUT WHICH MOVES AND FIGHTING POKÉMON GAMESWARRIOR THINKS ARE THE STRONGEST!

FIGHTING MOVES

CLOSE COMBAT

WHAT IT DOES: A fierce barrage of punches and kicks that's super powerful but slightly lowers the user's defences.

GamesWarrior's Verdict: This move is incredible because it shows the true power of Fighting types, even though it's a bit risky!

 ★★★★★

DYNAMIC PUNCH

WHAT IT DOES: A super strong punch that always confuses the opponent if it hits.

GamesWarrior's Verdict: It's like throwing a knockout punch that leaves the other Pokémon dizzy!

 ★★★★☆

BRICK BREAK

WHAT IT DOES: Smashes through barriers like Light Screen and Reflect, and then hits.

GamesWarrior's Verdict: This move is great because it breaks through defences and shows that nothing can stop a Fighting type!

 ★★★★☆

CROSS CHOP

WHAT IT DOES: Delivers a critical chop with a high chance of a critical hit.

GamesWarrior's Verdict: It's like cutting down the competition with a single powerful move!

 ★★★★☆

AURA SPHERE

WHAT IT DOES: Fires a blast of energy that never misses.

GamesWarrior's Verdict: This move is awesome because it shows the focused energy of Fighting types and always hits its mark!

 ★★★★★

FIGHTING POKÉMON

MACHAMP

ALL ABOUT: Machamp has four strong arms that can deliver a flurry of punches instantly.

STRENGTHS: It's incredibly strong and can move heavy objects that people can't lift.

GamesWarrior's Verdict: Machamp is a powerhouse in battles, perfect for anyone who likes a tough and reliable fighter.

 ★★★★☆

LUCARIO

ALL ABOUT: Lucario can sense its opponent's feelings and movements, which makes it a wise and strong fighter.

STRENGTHS: It mixes its Fighting skills with mystical Aura powers.

GamesWarrior's Verdict: Lucario is amazing because it combines physical power with spiritual energy, making it a unique and powerful fighter.

 ★★★★★

HITMONLEE

ALL ABOUT: Hitmonlee's legs stretch incredibly long, allowing it to deliver devastating kicks from a distance.

STRENGTHS: Known for its incredible kicking ability and flexibility.

GamesWarrior's Verdict: Hitmonlee is like a spring-loaded cannon of kicks, perfect for knocking out opponents!

 ★★★☆☆

BLAZIKEN

ALL ABOUT: Blaziken can leap over tall buildings and deliver fiery kicks and punches.

STRENGTHS: It mixes Fighting skills with Fire-type attacks, making it versatile in battles.

GamesWarrior's Verdict: A fiery fighter that brings heat to every battle, making it a fierce and exciting Pokémon to watch.

 ★★★★★

HOWLUCHA

ALL ABOUT: Hawlucha is a small but mighty Pokémon that uses its flying skills to enhance its Fighting moves.

STRENGTHS: It's quick and agile, making it hard to catch and hit.

GamesWarrior's Verdict: Hawlucha is like a high-flying wrestler, making it a fun and unpredictable fighter.

 ★★★★☆

CONKELDURR

ALL ABOUT: Conkeldurr holds a concrete pillar in each hand, which it uses to smash its opponents.

STRENGTHS: It's incredibly strong and uses its concrete pillars to deliver powerful blows.

GamesWarrior's Verdict: Conkeldurr is like a construction worker turned superhero, using its strength to overcome any challenge.

 ★★★☆☆

What GamesWarrior loves most!

Fighting Pokémon are all about courage and power, making every battle exciting and full of action! GamesWarrior's favourite is Lucario because it has strong fighting skills and uses its Aura to understand and outsmart opponents.

LET'S TALK ABOUT... POISON TYPES

POISON TYPES are the crafty alchemists of the Pokémon world, wielding toxic powers to control and conquer their battles! They utilise venomous moves like Sludge Bomb and Toxic that can debilitate opponents over time. Poison types are particularly effective against Grass and Fairy types, showcasing their ability to disrupt and damage using nature's more sinister side. They need to be cautious around Ground, Psychic, and Steel types, which can resist or are immune to their toxic tricks. Pokémon like Gengar and Muk are like the venomous vanguards of Poison Pokémon because they blend potency with persistence.

LET'S EXPLORE WHICH MOVES AND POISON POKÉMON GAMESWARRIOR THINKS ARE THE MOST LETHAL!

POISON MOVES

SLUDGE BOMB

WHAT IT DOES: Hurls a ball of toxic sludge that may poison the target.

GamesWarrior's Verdict: This move is explosively effective, combining strong immediate impact with the chance to poison, hindering foes over time!

★★★★☆

TOXIC

WHAT IT DOES: Badly poisons the target, increasing the poison damage every turn.

GamesWarrior's Verdict: It's a quintessential poison move that embodies the slow and sinister nature of poisoning, becoming more dangerous as the battle drags on.

★★★★★

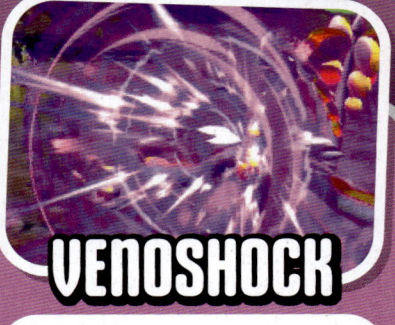

VENOSHOCK

WHAT IT DOES: Deals double damage to opponents that are already poisoned.

GamesWarrior's Verdict: This move is perfect for strategic battlers who can capitalise on worsening the state of their poisoned foes.

★★★★☆

CROSS POISON

WHAT IT DOES: A slashing attack with a high critical-hit ratio and a chance to poison.

GamesWarrior's Verdict: It's a cunningly sharp move that can turn the tides with critical hits and toxic effects.

★★★★☆

GUNK SHOT

WHAT IT DOES: Throws a lump of garbage at the target, with a high chance of poisoning.

GamesWarrior's Verdict: This move is surprisingly powerful, showing that sometimes even trash can be a treasure in battle with its strong impact and poisoning potential.

★★★★☆

POISON POKÉMON

GENGAR

ALL ABOUT: Gengar, the shadow Pokémon, lurks in the dark, using mischievous tricks to poison and confuse its enemies.

STRENGTHS: Known for its cunning nature and ability to seep into the shadows.

GamesWarrior's Verdict: Gengar epitomizes the sinister aspect of Poison types, using stealth and poison to outsmart opponents.

MUK

ALL ABOUT: Muk thrives in filth and sludge, becoming more potent and toxic as it absorbs pollution.

STRENGTHS: Its body is a poisonous ooze that can dissolve anything, making it dangerous to touch.

GamesWarrior's Verdict: Muk is a living hazard, capable of enduring harsh conditions while weakening foes with its very presence.

NIDOKING

ALL ABOUT: Nidoking uses its horn to inject deadly toxins and can smash boulders with its tail.

STRENGTHS: Combines physical strength with toxic abilities, making it a versatile and formidable foe.

GamesWarrior's Verdict: Nidoking is like a toxic king of the battlefield, ruling with power and poison.

CROBAT

ALL ABOUT: Crobat swoops silently, striking before its enemies are aware and using its fangs to deliver venom.

STRENGTHS: Known for its incredible speed and aerial agility.

GamesWarrior's Verdict: A deadly combination of speed and stealth, Crobat delivers quick and venomous strikes.

TOXICROAK

ALL ABOUT: Toxicroak lures in foes with the croaking sounds it produces, then lashes out with sharp claws and a poisonous jab.

STRENGTHS: It is particularly adept at using its poisonous abilities in close combat.

GamesWarrior's Verdict: Toxicroak is a fighter, thriving on its cunning and brutality, using poison as a weapon in its attacks.

WHO'S YOUR FAVOURITE POISON POKÉMON? MAYBE THE TRICKY GENGAR OR THE ENDURING MUK? POISON POKÉMON SURELY KNOW HOW TO LEAVE A LASTING IMPRESSION!

What GAMESWARRIOR loves most!

Poison Pokémon are the devious tacticians of the Pokémon universe, always finding ways to weaken their opponents and control the battlefield! GamesWarrior's favourite is Gengar for its blend of ghostly powers and toxic tricks, making it a dangerously delightful opponent.

LET'S TALK ABOUT... GROUND TYPES

GROUND TYPES are the rugged and powerful Pokémon that dominate the terrain! They control moves like **Earthquake** and **Dig** that shake up the battlefield and undermine their opponents. Ground types are superb at tackling Electric, Fire, Poison, Rock, and Steel types, demonstrating their mastery over the land. But they must watch out for Water, Grass, and Ice types, which can disrupt their solid footing. Pokémon like **Groudon** and **Excadrill** are like the earth movers of Ground Pokémon because they're so strong and dependable.

LET'S DIG INTO WHICH MOVES AND GROUND POKÉMON GAMESWARRIOR THINKS ARE THE STURDIEST!

GROUND MOVES

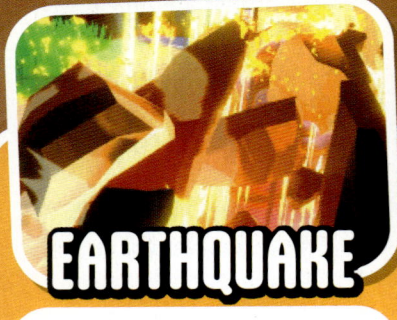

EARTHQUAKE

WHAT IT DOES: Causes a massive tremor that affects all Pokémon on the ground.

GamesWarrior's Verdict: This move is earth-shattering because it delivers a powerful shock to everyone around, making it a game-changer in many battles!

★★★★★

DIG

WHAT IT DOES: The user burrows underground on the first turn, then pops up to strike on the second turn.

GamesWarrior's Verdict: It's clever because you can hide from an attack and then surprise your opponent with a strong hit!

★★★★☆

MUD SHOT

WHAT IT DOES: Hurls mud at the opponent, lowering their speed.

GamesWarrior's Verdict: This move is great for slowing down fast opponents, giving you a muddy but effective advantage.

★★★☆☆

BULLDOZE

WHAT IT DOES: Stomps around to create a mini-earthquake that reduces others' speed.

GamesWarrior's Verdict: It's like taking control of the battlefield by shaking up everything and everyone in your path!

★★★★★

SAND TOMB

WHAT IT DOES: Traps the opponent in a swirling vortex of sand for several turns, causing continuous damage.

GamesWarrior's Verdict: A powerful move because it keeps hurting your opponent over time, like quicksand that won't let go.

★★★☆☆

GROUND POKÉMON

GROUDON

ALL ABOUT: Groudon is said to have expanded the lands by evaporating water with its heat.

STRENGTHS: It has immense power and can cause volcanic eruptions.

GamesWarrior's Verdict: Groudon is like the titan of the land, with the ability to shape the earth and challenge any opponent.

 ★★★★★

EXCADRILL

ALL ABOUT: Excadrill can tunnel through the ground at high speeds and emerge for powerful attacks.

STRENGTHS: Known for its drilling capabilities that can even break through steel.

GamesWarrior's Verdict: Excadrill is fantastic for its speed and power, making it a fearsome fighter underground and above.

 ★★★★☆

KROOKODILE

ALL ABOUT: Krookodile intimidates its foes with its glaring eyes and can crunch anything with its powerful jaws.

STRENGTHS: It's aggressive and has versatile abilities that make it a formidable opponent.

GamesWarrior's Verdict: Krookodile is like the outlaw of the desert, tough and relentless in pursuit of victory.

 ★★★★☆

FLYGON

ALL ABOUT: Flygon stirs up sandstorms with wings and can disappear into the desert winds.

STRENGTHS: It is elusive and can navigate any sandstorm.

GamesWarrior's Verdict: Flygon is like a guardian of the desert with the ability to command the sands.

 ★★★☆☆

MAMOSWINE

ALL ABOUT: Mamoswine ploughs through snow and ice with its massive tusks, surviving in cold terrains where others cannot.

STRENGTHS: It's incredibly sturdy and resilient in harsh conditions.

GamesWarrior's Verdict: It's like a prehistoric powerhouse, capable of enduring and thriving in the toughest environments.

 ★★★☆☆

RHYPERIOR

ALL ABOUT: Rhyperior can shoot rocks from its hands and is nearly unbeatable in physical combat.

STRENGTHS: Its rock-hard armour makes it nearly immune to physical attacks.

GamesWarrior's Verdict: Rhyperior is like a walking fortress, unyielding and unstoppable on the battlefield.

 ★★★★☆

Ground Pokémon are the foundation of any team, providing strength and stability with their deep connection to the earth! GamesWarrior's favourite is Groudon, which is legendary in name and reputation for its ability to shape landscapes and dominate battles.

LET'S TALK ABOUT...

FLYING TYPES

FLYING TYPES are the high-flyers of the Pokémon world, soaring above the rest with grace and speed! They have aerial moves like **Aerial Ace** and **Sky Attack** that showcase their mastery of the skies. Flying types are especially effective against Grass, Bug, and Fighting types, swooping in with the advantage of altitude. But they must watch out for Electric, Ice, and Rock types, which can ground them fast. Pokémon like **Pidgeot** and **Braviary** are like the aces of Flying Pokémon because they command the sky with power and precision.

LET'S EXPLORE WHICH MOVES AND FLYING POKÉMON GAMESWARRIOR THINKS SOAR THE HIGHEST!

FLYING MOVES

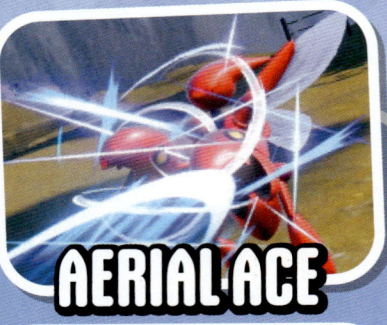

AERIAL ACE

WHAT IT DOES: A swift and sure strike that never misses its target.

GamesWarrior's Verdict: This move is brilliant because it's like having perfect aim every time you swoop in for the attack!

GW RATING ★★★★☆

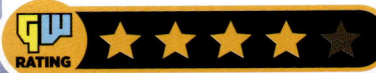

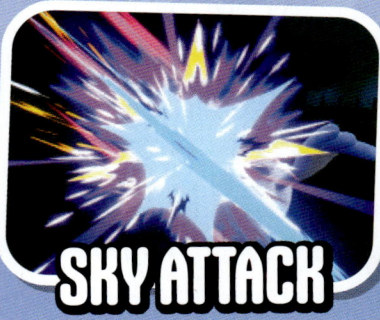

SKY ATTACK

WHAT IT DOES: Charges up a powerful hit on the first turn, then strikes with massive force on the second.

GamesWarrior's Verdict: It's like drawing back a bowstring to release a powerful arrow that zooms across the sky!

GW RATING ★★★★★

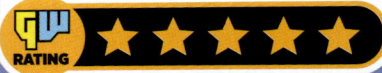

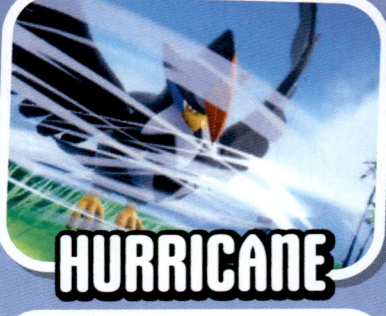

HURRICANE

WHAT IT DOES: Whips up a fierce storm that can confuse the opponent.

GamesWarrior's Verdict: This move is incredible because it's like summoning a wild storm to disorient and batter your foes!

GW RATING ★★★★☆

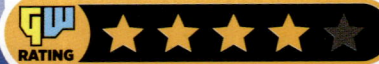

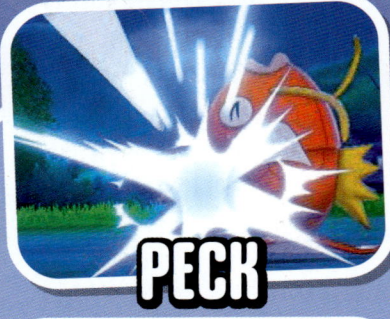

PECK

WHAT IT DOES: A quick and simple stab with a beak or similar appendage.

GamesWarrior's Verdict: It's a basic but effective way to peck at your opponent, showing that sometimes simple is best!

GW RATING ★★★☆☆

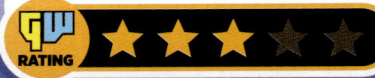

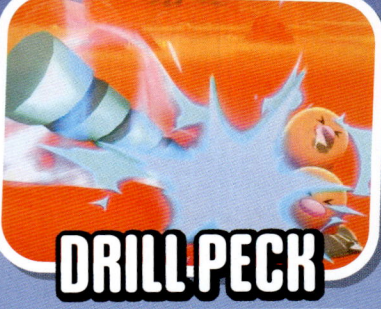

DRILL PECK

WHAT IT DOES: A stronger, spinning version of Peck that delivers multiple hits rapidly.

GamesWarrior's Verdict: This move is awesome because it's like turning into a living drill, boring into opponents with force!

GW RATING ★★★★☆

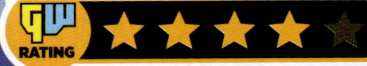

FLYING POKÉMON

PIDGEOT

ALL ABOUT: Pidgeot can reach incredible speeds and has a majestic appearance.

STRENGTHS: Known for its speed and precision in flight.

GamesWarrior's Verdict: Pidgeot is a classic, using its speed and sharp vision to dominate the skies.

★★★★☆

BRAVIARY

ALL ABOUT: Braviary symbolises courage and strength and is known for its fearless flights.

STRENGTHS: It's incredibly brave and can carry heavy loads while flying.

GamesWarrior's Verdict: Braviary is like the superhero of the skies, bold and unbending in the face of danger.

★★★★★

STARAPTOR

ALL ABOUT: Staraptor strikes fiercely and is known for its intimidating demeanour.

STRENGTHS: It combines speed with powerful attacking moves.

GamesWarrior's Verdict: Staraptor is intense, diving into battle with all its might and scaring its enemies with its fierce cries.

★★★★☆

NOCTOWL

ALL ABOUT: Noctowl can see perfectly in the dark and is known for its wise appearance.

STRENGTHS: It's intelligent and stealthy, making it a master of nighttime hunting.

GamesWarrior's Verdict: Noctowl is like the wise old owl of Pokémon, using its smarts and stealth to outwit opponents.

★★★☆☆

ALTARIA

ALL ABOUT: Altaria sings enchanting melodies as it glides peacefully in the sky.

STRENGTHS: Its songs can soothe, and its fluffy feathers are like clouds.

GamesWarrior's Verdict: Altaria brings beauty and calm to the battle, making it as soothing as it is strong.

★★★★☆

TALONFLAME

ALL ABOUT: Talonflame combines the ferocity of fire with the swiftness of flight.

STRENGTHS: It's incredibly fast and strikes with fiery attacks.

GamesWarrior's Verdict: Talonflame is like a meteor, blazing through the sky with incredible speed and fiery power.

★★★★★

What GamesWarrior loves most!

Flying Pokémon capture the freedom of the skies and the thrill of the wind beneath their wings! GamesWarrior's top pick is Braviary for its inspiring courage and awe-inspiring flights.

LET'S TALK ABOUT... PSYCHIC TYPES

PSYCHIC TYPES are the profound strategists of the Pokémon world, wielding extraordinary mental powers to outthink and overpower their foes! They utilise moves like **Psychic** and **Psyshock** that harness the mind's potential to cause damage and manipulate the battlefield. Psychic types excel against Fighting and Poison types, showcasing their ability to overcome physical strength and toxicity with sheer mental prowess. Whilst Bug, Ghost, and Dark types can break their defences, Pokémon like **Alakazam** and **Espeon** are like the cerebral champions of Psychic Pokémon, combining intellect with intense psychic energy.

LET'S EXPLORE WHICH MOVES AND PSYCHIC POKÉMON GAMESWARRIOR THINKS ARE THE MOST MIND-BENDING!

PSYCHIC MOVES

PSYCHIC

WHAT IT DOES: Harnesses psychic power to strike the target, possibly lowering their Special Defence.

GamesWarrior's Verdict: This move is classic, perfect for delivering both physical and mental blows, showcasing the iconic power of Psychic types!

★★★★★

PSYSHOCK

WHAT IT DOES: Deals damage based on the opponent's Defense instead of Special Defense, confusing their usual protective measures.

GamesWarrior's Verdict: A clever twist in attack strategy, ideal for bypassing foes prepared against typical psychic assaults.

★★★★☆

FUTURE SIGHT

WHAT IT DOES: Hits the opponent with a psychic attack two turns after it's used, predicting where the opponent will be.

GamesWarrior's Verdict: This move showcases the forethought and planning that Psychic types are famous for, striking from the future with pinpoint accuracy.

★★★★★

CALM MIND

WHAT IT DOES: Raises the user's Special Attack and Special Defense by focusing the mind.

GamesWarrior's Verdict: It's a powerful tool for self-enhancement, reflecting the inner strength and serenity of Psychic types.

★★★★☆

TELEKINESIS

WHAT IT DOES: It makes hitting the opponent easier by levitating them for a few turns.

GamesWarrior's Verdict: This move manipulates the battlefield to the Psychic type's advantage, showcasing their control over physical and mental spaces.

★★★★☆

PSYCHIC POKÉMON

ALAKAZAM

ALL ABOUT: Alakazam wields incredible intelligence and potent psychic powers, using its spoons to amplify its abilities.

STRENGTHS: Known for its astoundingly high IQ and fast reaction times, making it a formidable mind-bender.

GamesWarrior's Verdict: Alakazam is the epitome of Psychic prowess, manipulating both time and space with its profound psychic abilities.

GW Rating: ★★★★★

ESPEON

ALL ABOUT: Espeon evolves from Eevee through a deep bond with its trainer, developing sun-powered psychic skills.

STRENGTHS: It can predict the immediate future to dodge attacks and respond to threats preemptively.

GamesWarrior's Verdict: Espeon is a beacon of synchronicity and foresight, using its predictive powers to gracefully navigate battles.

GW Rating: ★★★★☆

METAGROSS

ALL ABOUT: Metagross uses its four brains to analyse and strategize, effectively outthinking its opponents.

STRENGTHS: Combines physical bulk with intellectual might, making it a dual threat on the battlefield.

GamesWarrior's Verdict: Metagross is like a supercomputer with limbs, calculating and executing strategies with cold precision.

GW Rating: ★★★★★

GARDEVOIR

ALL ABOUT: Gardevoir can sense its trainer's feelings and create small black holes using psychic energy to protect them.

STRENGTHS: Its empathetic nature is matched only by its powerful psychic abilities.

GamesWarrior's Verdict: Gardevoir is fiercely protective and elegantly powerful, embodying the emotional depth and strength of Psychic types.

GW Rating: ★★★★☆

LATIOS & LATIAS

ALL ABOUT: These Legendary Pokémon can telepathically communicate and fly at jet speeds, wrapped in a protective psychic field.

STRENGTHS: They blend high-speed flight with psychic and telepathic abilities, allowing them to act swiftly and smartly in any situation.

GamesWarrior's Verdict: Latios and Latias represent the perfect harmony of heart and mind, soaring above challenges with grace and tactical prowess.

GW Rating: ★★★★☆

?

WHO'S YOUR FAVOURITE PSYCHIC POKÉMON? MAYBE THE BRILLIANT ALAKAZAM OR THE STRATEGIC METAGROSS? PSYCHIC POKÉMON SURELY KNOW HOW TO DOMINATE THE MIND GAME!

♥ What GAMESWARRIOR loves most!

Psychic Pokémon mesmerize the battlefield with their deep strategic capabilities and overwhelming psychic powers! GamesWarrior's favourite is Metagross for its hybrid prowess as both a thinker and a warrior, genuinely representing the intellectual dominance of Psychic types.

LET'S TALK ABOUT... BUG TYPES

BUG TYPES are the underappreciated strategists of the Pokémon world, using their cunning and diverse abilities to outsmart and outlast opponents! They have moves like X-Scissor and Infestation that showcase their unique approach to combat, combining subtle strength with surprising tactics. Bug types excel against Grass, Psychic, and Dark types, showcasing their ability to exploit weaknesses in the natural order. However, they must be cautious around Fire, Flying, and Rock types, which can swiftly overcome their defences. Pokémon like Scizor and Volcarona are like the tactical masters of Bug Pokémon because they blend raw power with intricate strategies.

LET'S DIVE INTO WHICH MOVES AND BUG POKÉMON GAMESWARRIOR THINKS ARE THE MOST EFFECTIVE!

BUG MOVES

X-SCISSOR
WHAT IT DOES: Delivers a quick and sharp cross-cut that rarely misses.

GamesWarrior's Verdict: This move is perfect for swift and precise strikes, easily cutting through the competition!

GW RATING: ★★★★☆

INFESTATION
WHAT IT DOES: Traps the opponent in a swarm of tiny bugs, causing continuous damage over time.

GamesWarrior's Verdict: It's a great tactical move, slowly weakening the foe while preventing escape, embodying the persistent nature of Bug types.

GW RATING: ★★★★☆

BUG BUZZ
WHAT IT DOES: Emits a destructive sound wave that may lower the opponent's Special Defense.

GamesWarrior's Verdict: Using the power of sound to disrupt and damage, proving that Bug types can pack a surprising punch!

GW RATING: ★★★★★

SIGNAL BEAM
WHAT IT DOES: Fires a beam of light that can confuse the target.

GamesWarrior's Verdict: It's not just about damage; it's about disorienting the opponent, making it a multifaceted attack perfect for complex battle strategies.

GW RATING: ★★★★☆

LEECH LIFE
WHAT IT DOES: Drains the life force from the opponent, restoring the user's health.

GamesWarrior's Verdict: A brilliantly vampiric move that sustains the user while weakening the foe, ideal for long-lasting battles.

GW RATING: ★★★★☆

BUG POKÉMON

SCIZOR

ALL ABOUT: Scizor is a sleek and powerful Pokémon that uses its steel-hard claws to crush opponents.

STRENGTHS: Known for its incredible speed and strength, especially after evolving from Scyther.

GamesWarrior's Verdict: Combining brute force with metallic resilience, making Scizor a formidable foe in any battle scenario.

GW RATING: ★★★★★

VOLCARONA

ALL ABOUT: Volcarona uses its fiery wings to scatter burning scales capable of incinerating fields.

STRENGTHS: It can unleash powerful fire-based moves, unusual for Bug types.

GamesWarrior's Verdict: Volcarona is like a solar deity among bugs, bringing light and flame in darkness.

GW RATING: ★★★★★

HERACROSS

ALL ABOUT: Heracross uses its oversized horn to toss foes in the air, relying on brute strength.

STRENGTHS: Combines a Beetle's power with a wrestler's strategy.

GamesWarrior's Verdict: Heracross uses its environment and physical prowess to beat opponents.

GW RATING: ★★★★☆

BEEDRILL

ALL ABOUT: Beedrill is aggressive and swift, attacking with venomous stingers on its forelimbs and tail.

STRENGTHS: It strikes quickly and retreats before the opponent can counterattack.

GamesWarrior's Verdict: Representing the hit-and-run tactics that are core to Bug-type strategies, making it a fearsome striker.

GW RATING: ★★★☆☆

BUTTERFREE

ALL ABOUT: Butterfree uses its wings to spread highly toxic pollen and can soothe foes to sleep.

STRENGTHS: Excels in status effects, manipulating battles to their favour.

GamesWarrior's Verdict: Butterfree demonstrates that power in the Pokémon world isn't just about brute force but also about control and finesse.

GW RATING: ★★★☆☆

?

WHO'S YOUR FAVOURITE BUG POKÉMON? MAYBE THE MIGHTY SCIZOR OR THE FIERY VOLCARONA? BUG POKÉMON SURELY HAVE A WAY OF CREEPING INTO YOUR FAVOUR!

♥ What GAMESWARRIOR loves most!

Bug Pokémon showcase that success in battle often requires brains over brawn, and their diverse abilities make them unpredictable and versatile! GamesWarrior's favourite is Volcarona for its majestic presence and unique ability to bring fire into play, illuminating the often-overlooked power of Bug types.

LET'S TALK ABOUT LEGENDARY POKÉMON

EVERYONE HAS THEIR OWN FAVOURITES, BUT WE THINK WE'VE GOT AT LEAST ONE TRAINER'S DREAM TEAM RIGHT HERE. HERE'S A RUNDOWN OF GAMESWARRIOR'S TOP FIVE LEGENDARY POKÉMON AND WHY.

Legendary Pokémon are more than cool monsters on the box cover; they're often the focus of the story and come jam-packed with ridiculously powerful moves and overpowered statistics. They're usually very challenging to get, with experienced trainers saving their Master Ball for a guaranteed catch. **GamesWarrior** is going to look at every Legendary from every generation and give you our top picks.

WHICH ONE IS YOUR FAVOURITE?

GAMESWARRIOR'S TOP 5 LEGENDARY POKÉMON

5 ZYGARDE

Zygarde monitors the ecosystem and can appear in various forms depending on how much power is needed. In its Complete Form, it's known as the guardian of the environment!

GW RATING: ★★★★☆

Zygarde's adaptability and its role as the protector of the ecosystem make it a unique and formidable Pokémon.

4 GROUDON

As the Continent Pokémon, Groudon can summon intense sunlight to heat up battles. It also clashes with its aquatic counterpart, Kyogre, shaping the land and seas.

GW RATING: ★★★★☆

With the power to expand continents under its control, Groudon packs a punch that's hard to beat in any terrain.

3 LUGIA

Guardian of the seas, Lugia can calm storms with a flap of its wings. Known as the 'Beast of the Sea', it is as mysterious as the ocean depths.

GW RATING: ★★★★☆

Lugia's potent combination of Psychic and Flying powers, along with its majestic presence, makes it a favourite among legendary enthusiasts.

2 MEWTWO

Created from Mew's DNA, this Psychic-type Pokémon possesses formidable intelligence and psychic abilities, making it one of the most powerful Pokémon ever.

GW RATING: ★★★★☆

Mewtwo's raw power and the dramatic story of its creation capture the imagination, making it a top choice for any battle.

1 RAYQUAZA

Rayquaza lives in the Earth's ozone layer, only descending to quell the feuds of Groudon and Kyogre. It has a unique ability to Mega Evolve without needing a Mega Stone, showcasing its true sky-high potential.

GW RATING: ★★★★★

Rayquaza's command over the skies and its game-changing Mega Evolution earn it the top spot as the most awe-inspiring legendary Pokémon!

GAMESWARRIOR'S VERDICT

Legendary Pokémon are rare and powerful creatures that trainers highly desire due to their unique abilities and strength. However, catching them can be difficult without a Master Ball, which has a 100% capture rate. If trainers do not have a Master Ball, catching a legendary Pokémon can be a challenging and time-consuming task. But, the reward of having a legendary creature on your team is worth the effort.

TOP 5 GAMESWARRIOR'S MYTHICAL

Mythical Pokémon are even rarer to find than Legendary Pokémon! Some trainers dedicate their whole lives to catching a glimpse of these rare Pocket Monsters, with some even having the power to control the weather, time and even humans or other Pokémon. Here's a breakdown of GamesWarrior's favourite Mythical Pokémon.

5 DARKRAI

FUN TRIVIA: Darkrai is featured in its own movie, 'Pokémon: The Rise of Darkrai', where it plays a hero's role, unlike its usual mysterious and somewhat frightening persona in the games.

GW RATING: ★★★★☆

GamesWarrior's Verdict: Catching Darkrai requires overcoming its nightmarish challenges and understanding its true protective nature, offering a deeply engaging and thrilling quest.

4 ARCEUS

FUN TRIVIA: Arceus has the highest base stat total of all Mythical Pokémon and is involved in Sinnoh's creation myth, making it integral to the region's folklore.

GW RATING: ★★★★★

GamesWarrior's Verdict: Arceus presents an almost divine challenge, combining immense power with deep lore, making it a monumental capture for any dedicated Trainer.

3 JIRACHI

FUN TRIVIA: Jirachi is inspired by the concept of Tanabata, a Japanese star festival where people make wishes that are believed to come true — a fitting theme for a wish-granting Pokémon.

GW RATING: ★★★★☆

GamesWarrior's Verdict: The brief awakening of Jirachi every thousand years makes each encounter incredibly rare, and the opportunity to make a wish adds a magical touch to the challenge.

POKÉMON

2 CELEBI

FUN TRIVIA: Celebi has a starring role in the fourth Pokémon movie, 'Celebi: Voice of the Forest', where it travels through time to prevent its own demise and ensure the safety of the forest.

★★★★★

GamesWarrior's Verdict: Celebi's unique ability to travel through time and its guardianship of nature create an enchanting yet formidable task for Trainers seeking to catch it.

1 MEW

FUN TRIVIA: Mew was not originally intended to be part of the Pokémon Red and Green games. Its creator, Shigeki Morimoto, secretly added it as a little extra without any plans to reveal it officially.

★★★★★

GamesWarrior's Verdict: Mew's elusive nature and the mystery of its existence make catching this Pokémon a legendary feat, filled with wonder and excitement.

GAMESWARRIOR'S VERDICT

Mythical Pokémon are unique and very rare Pokémon that you can't find anywhere in the game! To try and get one, trainers must keep an eye out for special Pokémon events that happen occasionally, either in-person or online via Mystery Gift. They are usually given out during special Pokémon events. Pokémon like Mew, Celebi, and Jirachi are part of this group and are all very unique. Catching these Pokémon is exciting and makes Pokémon adventures even more fun!

LET'S TALK ABOUT...

ROCK TYPES

ROCK TYPES are the stalwart defenders and rugged battlers of the Pokémon world, standing firm against many challenges with their solid resilience! They wield powerful moves like **Stone Edge** and **Rock Slide** that capitalise on their stony strength to crush opponents. Rock types are particularly effective against Fire, Ice, Flying, and Bug types, showcasing their ability to shatter and grind down foes. Water, Grass, Fighting, Ground, and Steel types can easily break their defences, but Pokémon like **Tyranitar** and **Golem** are hard-hitting Rock Pokémon because they blend immense durability with devastating power.

LET'S DELVE INTO WHICH MOVES AND ROCK POKÉMON GAMESWARRIOR THINKS ARE THE MOST FORMIDABLE!

ROCK MOVES

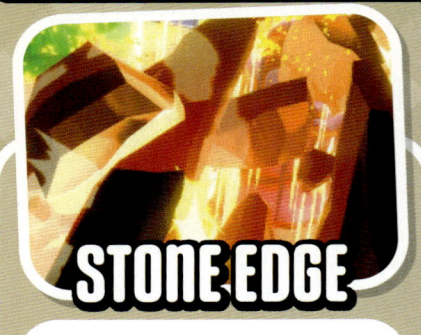

STONE EDGE
WHAT IT DOES: Delivers a sharp, sudden strike with a high critical-hit ratio.

GamesWarrior's Verdict: This move is a cornerstone for Rock types, offering sheer cutting power with a significant chance to land critical damage!

GW RATING: ★★★★★

ROCK SLIDE
WHAT IT DOES: Causes a landslide of rocks to hit multiple foes, potentially causing them to flinch.

GamesWarrior's Verdict: It's excellent for taking on multiple opponents, showing that Rock types can control the battlefield with overwhelming force.

GW RATING: ★★★★☆

ROCK WRECKER
WHAT IT DOES: It hits with massive force but requires recharging the next turn.

GamesWarrior's Verdict: This move is all about raw power, smashing anything in its path but needing a pause to gather strength again.

GW RATING: ★★★★☆

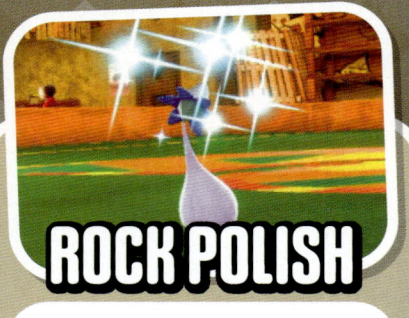

ROCK POLISH
WHAT IT DOES: Polishes the Pokémon's body to sharply raise its Speed stat.

GamesWarrior's Verdict: It's a tactical move that complements the typically slow nature of Rock types, giving them a surprising boost in agility.

GW RATING: ★★★★☆

SANDSTORM
WHAT IT DOES: Whips up a sandstorm that lasts several turns, damaging all types but Rock, Ground, and Steel.

GamesWarrior's Verdict: This move creates a harsh environment that plays to the strengths of Rock types, providing both defence and offence over time.

GW RATING: ★★★★☆

ROCK POKÉMON

TYRANITAR
ALL ABOUT: Tyranitar can alter the landscape by walking, causing small tremors and creating sandstorms.

STRENGTHS: Known for its incredible toughness and the ability to dish out substantial damage.

GamesWarrior's Verdict: Tyranitar stands as a titan among Rock types, nearly unstoppable once it gains momentum.

GW RATING: ★★★★★

GOLEM
ALL ABOUT: Golem can roll down slopes to gather speed and crush its foes under its massive weight.

STRENGTHS: Its rock-hard shell provides a formidable defence, making it a reliable tank in battle.

GamesWarrior's Verdict: Golem embodies the indomitable spirit of Rock types, using its bulk and power to endure and attack.

GW RATING: ★★★★★

ONIX
ALL ABOUT: Onix, resembling a giant chain of boulders, tunnels through the ground at high speed.

STRENGTHS: It can quickly create tunnels and use its length and size to intimidate foes.

GamesWarrior's Verdict: Onix is like a living fortress, using its massive size and strength to dominate the terrain.

GW RATING: ★★★☆☆

RHYPERIOR
ALL ABOUT: Rhyperior can shoot boulders from its arms, standing its ground against even the most formidable foes.

STRENGTHS: It has an incredible offensive and defensive capability, making it a powerhouse.

GamesWarrior's Verdict: Rhyperior is the artillery of Rock types, capable of withstanding severe attacks while retaliating with equal force.

GW RATING: ★★★★☆

AGGRON
ALL ABOUT: Aggron claims an entire mountain as its territory, fiercely defending it from intruders.

STRENGTHS: Its steel-hard armour makes it nearly invincible in direct combat.

GamesWarrior's Verdict: Aggron is like a knight in shining armour, protective and relentless in the defence of its domain.

GW RATING: ★★★★☆

? WHO'S YOUR FAVOURITE ROCK POKÉMON? MAYBE THE FORMIDABLE TYRANITAR OR THE STEADFAST GOLEM? ROCK POKÉMON SURELY KNOW HOW TO STAND FIRM AND DELIVER CRUSHING BLOWS!

♥ What GAMESWARRIOR loves most!
Rock Pokémon are the unyielding giants of the Pokémon universe, demonstrating that strength and resilience can often lead to victory! GamesWarrior's favourite is Tyranitar for its legendary ability to shape the environment to its advantage, making it a true force of nature.

LET'S TALK ABOUT...

GHOST TYPES

GHOST TYPES are the mysterious and spooky Pokémon that haunt the battlefields with their eerie powers! They wield chilling moves like Shadow Ball and Phantom Force that can sneak past defences and spook their opponents. Ghost types excel against other Ghost and Psychic types, revealing their ability to interact with the supernatural realm. However, they need to be cautious around Dark types, which can resist their spooky tactics. Pokémon like Gengar and Mimikyu are like the spectral masters of Ghost Pokémon because they blend fright and might seamlessly.

LET'S UNCOVER WHICH MOVES AND GHOST POKÉMON GAMESWARRIOR THINKS ARE THE MOST GHOSTLY!

GHOST MOVES

SHADOW BALL
WHAT IT DOES: Fires a blob of ghostly energy that might lower the opponent's defensive power.

GamesWarrior's Verdict: This move is fantastic because it's like throwing a haunted orb that can weaken and scare simultaneously!

GW RATING: ★★★★☆

PHANTOM FORCE
WHAT IT DOES: The user vanishes, then strikes back with a guaranteed hit next turn.

GamesWarrior's Verdict: It's like playing a game of hide and seek and then surprising your foe with a sneak attack!

GW RATING: ★★★★★

HEX
WHAT IT DOES: Deals more damage to opponents affected by a condition like being asleep or poisoned.

GamesWarrior's Verdict: This move is clever because it turns your opponent's bad luck into a greater nightmare!

GW RATING: ★★★★☆

OMINOUS WIND
WHAT IT DOES: A gust of repelling wind that can boost all the user's stats.

GamesWarrior's Verdict: It's like calling forth a ghostly wind that not only harms but can also empower the user mysteriously!

GW RATING: ★★★★☆

SPIRIT SHACKLE
WHAT IT DOES: A spectral arrow that prevents the opponent from escaping.

GamesWarrior's Verdict: A powerful move that is like trapping your opponent in a haunted house from which they can't escape!

GW RATING: ★★★★☆

GHOST POKÉMON

GENGAR

ALL ABOUT: Gengar loves to cast shadows and play tricks with its eerie powers.

STRENGTHS: Known for its mischievous nature and powerful ghostly attacks.

GamesWarrior's Verdict: Gengar is like the classic haunted ghost, always ready with a spooky trick up its sleeve.

GW RATING: ★★★★★

MIMIKYU

ALL ABOUT: Mimikyu wears a cloth to look like Pikachu so it can make friends because it's lonely.

STRENGTHS: Under its disguise, it harbours a desire to be loved and the power to fight back when threatened.

GamesWarrior's Verdict: Mimikyu is touching because it shows that even the spookiest Pokémon just want to be loved.

GW RATING: ★★★★☆

BANETTE

ALL ABOUT: Banette is a doll that became a Pokémon out of a strong desire for revenge.

STRENGTHS: It's driven by powerful emotions and can unleash incredible energy.

GamesWarrior's Verdict: Banette is fascinating as it turns its grudge into a source of power, showing that even in the Pokémon world, feelings matter.

GW RATING: ★★★☆☆

CHANDELURE

ALL ABOUT: Chandelure illuminates the dark by burning the spirits it absorbs.

STRENGTHS: It's mighty in trapping opponents and dealing damage over time.

GamesWarrior's Verdict: Chandelure is like a ghostly chandelier, casting light and shadows while harbouring eerie spirits.

GW RATING: ★★★★☆

SABLEYE

ALL ABOUT: Sableye scuttles through the shadows with its jewel eyes gleaming, scavenging for gems.

STRENGTHS: It's sneaky and durable, with an uncanny ability to avoid attacks.

GamseWarrior's Verdict: Sableye is intriguing because it shows that sometimes being a little different can be a good thing.

GW RATING: ★★★☆☆

DUSKNOIR

ALL ABOUT: Dusknoir communicates with the spirit world, guiding lost spirits home.

STRENGTHS: It's known as a conductor of souls and is both feared and respected.

GamesWarrior's Verdict: Dusknoir is like the guardian of the afterlife, ensuring peace and order among spirits.

GW RATING: ★★★★☆

♥ What GAMESWARRIOR loves most!

Ghost Pokémon enchant the battlefield with their mystical presence and tricky moves! GamesWarrior's top ghost is Gengar for its iconic status and knack for causing delightful frights.

LET'S TALK ABOUT...
DRAGON TYPES

DRAGON TYPES are some of the strongest and coolest Pokémon you can find! They have moves like Draco Meteor and Dragon Dance that show just how awesome they are. Dragons are super tough against other Dragons but have to watch out for Ice, Fairy, and other Dragons that can give them a hard time. Pokémon like Garchomp and Rayquaza are like the kings and queens of Dragon Pokémon because they're so powerful and amazing.

LET'S SEE WHAT MOVES AND DRAGON POKÉMON GAMESWARRIOR THINKS ARE THE BEST!

DRAGON MOVES

DRACO METEOR
WHAT IT DOES: This move is super strong, like a meteor falling from the sky!

GamesWarrior's Verdict: This move is amazing because it hits super hard, like a superhero's punch!

GW RATING: ★★★★★

DRAGON DANCE
WHAT IT DOES: It makes the Pokémon faster and stronger, and ready to win!

GamesWarrior's Verdict: This move is like a magic dance that makes you quick and powerful!

GW RATING: ★★★★★

OUTRAGE
WHAT IT DOES: Keeps attacking for a bit but then confuses the Pokémon.

GamesWarrior's Verdict: It's like throwing a wild tantrum that's super strong but makes you dizzy!

GW RATING: ★★★★★

DRAGON CLAW
WHAT IT DOES: A reliable attack is always good in a long battle.

GamesWarrior's Verdict: This move is like having super sharp claws that never miss!

GW RATING: ★★★★★

DRAGON PULSE
WHAT IT DOES: A strong and accurate energy blast.

GamesWarrior's Verdict: It's a cool energy wave that can hit from far away, really dependable!

GW RATING: ★★★★★

DRAGON POKÉMON

DRAGONITE

ALL ABOUT: Dragonite can do many things well, like flying fast and hitting hard with moves like 'Outrage'.

STRENGTHS: Dragonite is like a gentle giant but becomes super strong in battle!

GamesWarrior's Verdict: Dragonite is amazing for battles because it's tough and kind. It's like a big, friendly dragon that protects you.

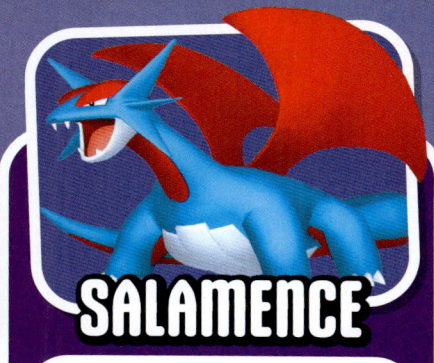

GW Rating: ★★★★☆

SALAMENCE

ALL ABOUT: Salamence can fly super fast and use 'Dragon Dance' to become even quicker and stronger.

STRENGTHS: When Salamence flies, it looks like a cool, fierce dragon zooming through the sky!

GamesWarrior's Verdict: Salamence is awesome because it zooms in the sky, and its "Dragon Dance" makes it super powerful.

GW Rating: ★★★★☆

GARCHOMP

ALL ABOUT: Garchomp can shake the ground with 'Earthquake' and has cool Dragon moves, too.

STRENGTHS: Garchomp is like a land-shark dragon that can cause mini-earthquakes!

GamesWarrior's Verdict: Garchomp is like a superhero because it's strong and can make many different moves.

GW Rating: ★★★★★

PALKIA

ALL ABOUT: Palkia has an extraordinary move, 'Spacial Rend', that's super powerful and unique.

STRENGTHS: Palkia can control space, which is like having the power to bend the air around it!

GamesWarrior's Verdict: Palkia is like a wizard dragon because it can do sapce magic and hit really hard.

GW Rating: ★★★★★

RAYQUAZA

ALL ABOUT: Rayquaza can evolve mega without needing a special stone, making it versatile.

STRENGTHS: Rayquaza watches over the sky and can fly higher than any plane!

GamesWarrior's Verdict: Rayquaza is the coolest because it's like the guardian of the sky and super strong.

GW Rating: ★★★★★

LATIOS & LATIAS

ALL ABOUT: These Pokémon are super fast and have psychic powers along with their dragon powers.

STRENGTHS: Latios and Latias can understand humans and have a strong bond with them.

GamesWarrior's Verdict: Latios and Latias are special because they're fast, smart, and care about their friends.

GW Rating: ★★★★☆

What GAMESWARRIOR loves most!

Dragon Pokémon are some of the coolest because of their amazing powers and strength in battles. Out of all of them, GamesWarrior loves Rayquaza the most because it's like the superhero of the sky, keeping watch over the world from way up high. It's super strong and can change shape, which is cool!

LET'S TALK ABOUT... DARK TYPES

DARK TYPES are the sneaky and clever Pokémon of the night! They have cool moves like **Crunch** and **Dark Pulse** that let them fight smart, not just hard. Dark types are great at battling against Psychic and Ghost types because they're masters of the shadows. But they must be careful around Fighting, Bug, and Fairy types. Pokémon like **Tyranitar** and **Umbreon** are like the shadowy protectors of Dark Pokémon because they're so strong and mysterious.

LET'S CHECK OUT WHICH MOVES AND DARK POKÉMON GAMESWARRIOR THINKS ARE THE COOLEST!

DARK MOVES

CRUNCH
WHAT IT DOES: Delivers a powerful bite that can weaken the other Pokémon by hurting their defence.
GamesWarrior's Verdict: This move is cool because it's like having super strong jaws!
GW RATING: ★★★★☆

DARK PULSE
WHAT IT DOES: Sends out a wave of dark energy that can make the opponent flinch.
GamesWarrior's Verdict: It's awesome because it's like shooting a shadow that can scare and stop other Pokémon!
GW RATING: ★★★★☆

FOUL PLAY
WHAT IT DOES: Uses the opponent's strength against them, which is pretty sneaky.
GamesWarrior's Verdict: This move is clever because you use the other Pokémon's power to win!
GW RATING: ★★★★★

KNOCK OFF
WHAT IT DOES: Hits the opponent and makes them drop their item, which can mess up their plan.
GamesWarrior's Verdict: It's like taking away a toy, which can be tricky and useful in a battle!
GW RATING: ★★★★★

SUCKER PUNCH
WHAT IT DOES: Hits first if the other Pokémon is trying to attack, which is a smart first move.
GamesWarrior's Verdict: This move is great because it's like surprising someone with a quick trick!
GW RATING: ★★★★☆

DARK POKÉMON

TYRANITAR
ALL ABOUT: Tyranitar is like a walking mountain that's super tough and can cause sandstorms.

STRENGTHS: It's strong and can take a lot of hits, making it hard to beat.

GamesWarrior's Verdict: Tyranitar is amazing in battles because it's like a giant that's hard to knock down.

GW RATING: ★★★★★

UMBREON
ALL ABOUT: Umbreon is like a shadowy guardian who can glow in the dark and is super loyal.

STRENGTHS: Good at defending and can also heal itself, making it last a long time in battle.

GamesWarrior's Verdict: Umbreon is special because it's not just strong, it's also a faithful friend in the dark.

GW RATING: ★★★★☆

WEAVILE
ALL ABOUT: Weavile is quick and sneaky, with sharp claws that can cut through anything.

STRENGTHS: It's one of the fastest Pokémon and can hit hard before the opponent knows what happened.

GamesWarrior's Verdict: Weavile is cool because it's like a ninja that can win battles with its speed and surprise attacks.

GW RATING: ★★★★☆

HYDREIGON
ALL ABOUT: Hydreigon is a fierce dragon that can shoot blasts from its three heads.

STRENGTHS: It's mighty and can attack from a distance, which scares a lot of other Pokémon.

GamesWarrior's Verdict: Hydreigon is awesome because it's like having a three-headed dragon on your team!

GW RATING: ★★★★☆

ABSOL
ALL ABOUT: Absol can sense when something wrong will happen and tries to warn people.

STRENGTHS: It's brave and has a powerful attack that can change the outcome of battles.

GamesWarrior's Verdict: Absol is like a hero who looks out for others and fights bravely when needed.

GW RATING: ★★★☆☆

HONCHKROW
ALL ABOUT: Honchkrow looks like a bossy crow and commands other bird Pokémon.

STRENGTHS: It's like the king of the night skies and can call on other Pokémon to help in battles.

GamesWarrior's Verdict: Honchkrow is cool because it's like having a boss that can gather a team to win battles.

GW RATING: ★★★☆☆

What GAMESWARRIOR loves most!
Dark Pokémon are super sneaky and have some of the coolest tricks up their sleeves! GamesWarrior loves Tyranitar the most because it's like an unstoppable force that can protect its friends and stand strong against anything.

LET'S TALK ABOUT... STEEL TYPES

STEEL TYPES are the armoured warriors of the Pokémon world, boasting incredible defence and powerful, precise attacks! They wield moves like 'METEOR MASH' and 'IRON HEAD' that capitalise on their metallic composition to deliver crushing blows. Steel types are particularly effective against ICE, ROCK, and FAIRY TYPES, showcasing their ability to break and withstand opponents with their hard exteriors. On the other hand, they need to watch out for Fire, Fighting, and Ground types, which can penetrate their tough defences. Pokémon like Metagross and Steelix are like the fortresses of Steel Pokémon because they combine impenetrable defence with formidable strength.

LET'S EXPLORE WHICH MOVES AND STEEL POKÉMON GAMESWARRIOR THINKS ARE THE MOST FORMIDABLE!

STEEL MOVES

METEOR MASH
WHAT IT DOES: Strikes with a meteor-like punch may also raise the user's Attack stat.
GamesWarrior's Verdict: This move is a powerhouse, delivering cosmic force with a chance to become even more potent mid-battle!
★★★★★

IRON HEAD
WHAT IT DOES: Slams the opponent with a hard, iron head, often causing them to flinch.
GamesWarrior's Verdict: It's ideal for those who value precision and power, giving Steel types a reliable and impactful attack.
★★★★★

FLASH CANNON
WHAT IT DOES: Fires a blast of concentrated energy, potentially lowering the opponent's Special Defense.
GamesWarrior's Verdict: This move showcases the high-tech warfare Steel types can engage in, combining force with finesse.
★★★★☆

STEEL BEAM
WHAT IT DOES: Unleashes a powerful beam of steel energy but recoils considerable damage to the user.
GamesWarrior's Verdict: It's like wielding a double-edged sword, offering devastating power at a significant cost, perfect for dire situations.
★★★☆☆

IRON DEFENSE
WHAT IT DOES: Hardens the body's surface to sharply boost the Defense stat.
GamesWarrior's Verdict: This move turns Steel types into veritable fortresses, greatly enhancing their already impressive durability.
★★★★★

STEEL POKÉMON

METAGROSS

ALL ABOUT: Metagross is a supercomputer Pokémon that can outthink and outlast its opponents with its four brains and immense psychic powers.

STRENGTHS: Combines intellectual prowess with physical strength, making it a dual battle threat.

GamesWarrior's Verdict: Metagross is the epitome of Steel types, blending brain and brawn for a tactical advantage unlike any other.

GW RATING: ★★★★★

STEELIX

ALL ABOUT: Steelix, evolved from Onix, is even tougher and can burrow deeper than any other Pokémon.

STRENGTHS: Its body is harder than any metal and can withstand extreme pressure, making it nearly invincible.

GamesWarrior's Verdict: Steelix is like the underground king, dominating with its sheer unyielding nature and ironclad defence.

GW RATING: ★★★★☆

SCIZOR

ALL ABOUT: Scizor uses its steel-hard claws to cut through any obstacle, relying on speed and stealth with its new metallic body.

STRENGTHS: It's lighter and faster than its pre-evolved form, with a typing that grants it numerous resistances.

GamesWarrior's Verdict: Scizor combines agility with armour, making it a versatile and deadly adversary in any combat scenario.

GW RATING: ★★★★☆

MAGNEZONE

ALL ABOUT: Magnezone hovers in the air using electromagnetic forces, attacking with powerful electric and steel moves.

STRENGTHS: It can trap opponents with its magnetic field, enhancing its strategic capabilities.

GamesWarrior's Verdict: Magnezone is like a futuristic weapon, deploying both magnetism and electricity to secure victory.

GW RATING: ★★★★☆

AGGRON

ALL ABOUT: Aggron claims an entire mountain as its territory and fiercely defends it from intruders.

STRENGTHS: Its steel armour can deflect any attack and repair itself by consuming iron ore.

GamesWarrior's Verdict: Aggron is the tank-like protector of its domain, formidable in its defence and relentless in its counterattacks.

GW RATING: ★★★☆☆

?

WHO'S YOUR FAVOURITE STEEL POKÉMON? MAYBE THE TACTICAL METAGROSS OR THE STALWART STEELIX? STEEL POKÉMON SURELY KNOW HOW TO HOLD THEIR GROUND AND STRIKE BACK WITH PRECISION!

What GAMESWARRIOR loves most!

Steel Pokémon are the indomitable forces of the Pokémon universe, demonstrating that the best offence is often a good defence! GamesWarrior's favourite is Metagross for its unmatched combination of psychic intellect and steel resilience.

LET'S TALK ABOUT...
FAIRY TYPES

FAIRY TYPES are the magical Pokémon that sprinkle a little bit of enchantment in every battle! They've got dazzling moves like Moonblast and Fairy Wind that can outshine the competition. Fairy types have a magical edge against Dragon, Fighting, and Dark types, showing that even the smallest can stand tall. Pokémon like Togekiss and Sylveon are like the guardians of the Fairy Pokémon world because they're so graceful and strong.

LET'S DISCOVER WHICH MOVES AND FAIRY POKÉMON GAMESWARRIOR FINDS THE MOST ENCHANTING

FAIRY MOVES

MOONBLAST
WHAT IT DOES: A beam of moonlight that's not only pretty but really powerful, too!

GamesWarrior's Verdict: This move is amazing because it's like calling down the moon to help in battle!

★★★★☆

FAIRY WIND
WHAT IT DOES: A gentle breeze that carries a surprising punch.

GamesWarrior's Verdict: It's cool because it looks soft but can really knock the wind out of opponents!

★★★☆☆

DAZZLING GLEAM
WHAT IT DOES: Shines a bright light that dazzles and damages multiple opponents.

GamesWarrior's Verdict: This move is great for lighting up the battle and taking on more than one Pokémon at a time!

★★★★☆

PLAY ROUGH
WHAT IT DOES: It looks cute but packs a serious wallop, and it might even weaken the other Pokémon.

GamesWarrior's Verdict: It's like playing a game that turns serious, showing you shouldn't judge by appearances!

★★★★★

DISARMING VOICE
WHAT IT DOES: A sweet sound that hits all opponents without missing.

GamesWarrior's Verdict: This move is wonderful because it's impossible to avoid, like a song you can't get out of your head!

★★★☆☆

FAIRY POKÉMON

TOGEKISS

ALL ABOUT: Togekiss flies on the wings of joy, spreading happiness wherever it goes.

STRENGTHS: It's known for bringing luck and can dodge attacks well!

GamesWarrior's Verdict: Togekiss is magical in battles because it makes everyone feel good while still being super tough.

GW RATING: ★★★★☆

SYLVEON

ALL ABOUT: Sylveon uses its ribbons to calm battles and wrap opponents in kindness.

STRENGTHS: Its charm can overpower even the fiercest opponents.

GamesWarrior's Verdict: Sylveon is amazing for its ability to win battles with grace and beauty.

GW RATING: ★★★★★

MIMIKYU

ALL ABOUT: Mimikyu wears a cloth to look like Pikachu and make friends.

STRENGTHS: It's brave, and its disguise lets it take a hit without getting hurt.

GamesWarrior's Verdict: Mimikyu is special because it shows it's what's inside that counts, making it a sneaky and heartfelt fighter.

GW RATING: ★★★★☆

GARDEVOIR

ALL ABOUT: Gardevoir can sense when its Trainer is in danger and creates black holes to protect them.

STRENGTHS: Its devotion and psychic powers make it a formidable ally.

GamesWarrior's Verdict: Gardevoir is like a knight in shining armour, always ready to defend its friends with incredible power.

GW RATING: ★★★★★

FLORGES

ALL ABOUT: Florges draws strength from flowers and cares deeply for beautiful gardens.

STRENGTHS: It has powerful healing abilities and can control the battlefield with floral magic.

GamesWarrior's Verdict: Enchanting Florges shows the power of nature and caring, making it a nurturing force in battles.

GW RATING: ★★★★☆

CLEFABLE

ALL ABOUT: Clefable is said to live in quiet, peaceful places and has a gentle heart.

STRENGTHS: Its ability to hear great distances lets it avoid danger, and it can perform powerful magical attacks.

GamesWarrior's Verdict: Clefable is wonderful because it's gentle yet strong, using its magical talents to protect and battle.

GW RATING: ★★★☆☆

What GAMESWARRIOR loves most!

Fairy Pokémon sprinkle the battle with a bit of magic and lots of power! Out of all of them, GamesWarrior is most enchanted by Sylveon for its ability to combine strength with grace in a way that captivates everyone.

LET'S TALK ABOUT PARADOX POKÉMON

Paradox Pokémon from Pokémon Scarlet and Violet are ancient and futuristic versions of well-known Pokémon, leaving a big bag of mystery for trainers. Where did they come from? Why are future Paradox Pokémon robots? We don't know but these unique Pokémon are super cool and packed with mysteries. Let's explore the coolest ones and see how they stack up with a GamesWarrior verdict.

TOP 5 PARADOX POKEMON

5 SLITHER WING

WHY IT'S TOP TIER: Its mix of prehistoric coolness and bug-like mystery makes it a standout Pokémon!

★★★★½

Discovering Slither Wing is like unearthing a real-life treasure from ancient times.

4 IRON JUGULIS

WHY IT'S TOP TIER: Iron Jugulis blends the ferocity of a dragon with the sleekness of future technology.

★★★★½

This Pokémon is a fearsome yet fascinating sight in the skies of Paldea.

3 GREAT TUSK

WHY IT'S TOP TIER: Its gigantic presence and ancient vibe make it a thrilling encounter!

★★★★

Seeing Great Tusk is like stepping back into a time when dinosaurs roamed the earth.

2 FLUTTER MANE

WHY IT'S TOP TIER: Flutter Mane's spooky elegance makes it a ghostly spectacle.

★★★★

Perfect for those who love a mix of charm and chill in their Pokémon adventures.

1 IRON TREADS

WHY IT'S TOP TIER: Fast and formidable, its ability to transform and zoom around makes it a powerhouse and a race champion in disguise.

★★★★

Iron Treads is like a Pokémon on wheels!

GUIDE TO REGIONAL ABILITIES

Trainers use special abilities like Z-Moves, Mega Evolutions, Dynamaxing/Gigantamaxing, and Terastallising to give their Pokémon an advantage in battles. These abilities unlock their full potential, add depth to battles, and look cool! Here's the **GamesWarrior** breakdown and verdict.

Z-MOVES

Z-Moves are super powerful attacks that Pokémon can use in battle. To unleash a Z-Move, your Pokémon needs to hold a special item called a Z-Crystal, which matches the type of move (like Fire or Water). When used, it performs a big, dramatic, strong move! It's like a Pokémon's ultimate move and can be used only once in each battle, so you must pick the perfect moment!

Z-Moves add excitement to battles with their unique animations and game-changing power. They let trainers show off their strategy skills by choosing the best time to strike with their mightiest move. It's like having a secret weapon!

GW RATING: ★★★★★☆

MEGA EVOLUTIONS

Mega Evolutions let certain Pokémon transform into an even more powerful version of themselves during battle. To Mega Evolve, a Pokémon needs to hold a special item called a Mega Stone. This super cool transformation boosts their powers and often changes their appearance! It lasts until the battle ends, making them stronger for a while.

Mega Evolutions are not just powerful, but they also look super cool! They add depth to picking your Pokémon team because only certain Pokémon can Mega Evolve. It makes old Pokémon feel new and exciting again with their new looks and stronger abilities.

GW RATING: ★★★★★

DYNAMAXING/GIGANTAMIXING

In the Galar region Pokémon can Dynamax, which means they grow incredibly huge and their moves become more powerful, called Max Moves. Some Pokémon can even use Gigantamax to change their appearance and use unique G-Max Moves. This giant form only lasts for three turns in a battle, so timing is everything!

Dynamaxing and Gigantamaxing make battles dramatic and visually stunning. They're a fun twist because they make you think about the best moment to turn your Pokémon into a giant with super-strong powers. Plus, seeing your Pokémon become so big is just really cool!

GW RATING: ★★★★½

TERASTALLISING

Terastallising is a new way to power up your Pokémon in the Paldea region. By using a Tera Orb, your Pokémon can Terastallise to take on a sparkling, gem-like appearance and gain a new type based on its Tera Type, which can be different from its original type. This can surprise your opponent because your Pokémon might change types after a battle!

Terastallising is exciting because it adds a surprise element to battles. It allows Pokémon to adapt and overcome weaknesses or gain strengths, which can turn the battle. It's like giving Pokémon a dazzling costume change that packs a punch!

GW RATING: ★★★★☆

LET'S TALK ABOUT GYM LEADERS

There are so many gym leaders across the Pokémon core games, it's hard to pick out who are the best. Luckily for trainers, **GamesWarrior** have has done just that.

LT. SURGE (GENERATION I)

GYM: VERMILION CITY GYM

Lt. Surge, the 'Lightning American', is a formidable Gym Leader and a character with a rich backstory as a war veteran. His gym puzzle involves a tricky series of switches, making your victory feel even more rewarding.

GW RATING: ★★★★☆

His challenging setup and high-voltage charisma electrify the Gym experience, offering trainers a jolt of excitement.

WHITNEY (GENERATION II)

GYM: GOLDENROD CITY GYM

Whitney is infamous for her Miltank, which has caused many trainers to struggle with its devastating Rollout attack. Her emotional reaction to losing is both memorable and relatable.

GW RATING: ★★★★★

Whitney adds a personal touch to the Gym challenge, making her defeat a memorable milestone for any trainer.

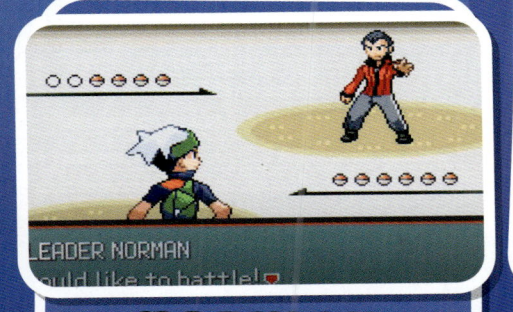

NORMAN (GENERATION III)

GYM: PETALBURG CITY GYM

Norman is unique because he's the player's father in the game, adding a layer of personal stakes to the challenge. His gym is structured around different room challenges, each with a battle style.

GW RATING: ★★★★½

The familial ties and innovative gym setup provide a compelling and heartwarming challenge.

VOLKNER (GENERATION IV)

GYM: SUNYSHORE CITY GYM

Volkner's passion for battling and his frustration with strong opponents make him a deeper, more introspective Gym Leader. His gym's puzzle involves moving platforms, adding an element of strategy to reach him.

GW RATING: ★★★★★

Volkner electrifies not just with his challenging gym puzzle but also his intense passion for battling.

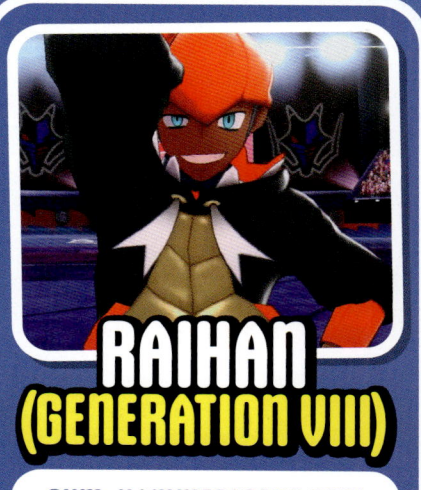

RAIHAN (GENERATION VIII)

GYM: HAMMERLOCKE GYM

Raihan is known for strategically using weather conditions in battles, offering a challenging twist on the typical Dragon-type encounter. His rivalry with the Champion adds an exciting competitive edge.

GW RATING: ★★★★½

Raihan breathes fire into the Gym Leader lineup with his innovative battle strategies and charismatic presence.

LET'S TALK ABOUT
POKÉMON TRADING CARD GAME

The Pokémon Trading Card Game (TCG) is not just about collecting and trading cool Pokémon cards — it also includes exciting events and new sets that keep the game fresh and fun. Let's dive into what kinds of sets and events you can find in the Pokémon TCG and see what GamesWarrior thinks about each one!

SET — NEW EXPANSION SETS

WHAT HAPPENS: Several times a year, new sets of cards are released. These sets often introduce new Pokémon, powerful moves, and sometimes even new ways to play the game!

GW RATING: ★★★★★

New sets are always exciting because they bring new strategies and cards to collect. It's like opening a treasure chest full of Pokémon surprises!

SET — SPECIAL COLLECTIONS

WHAT HAPPENS: Special collections often come out around specific themes or holidays and include unique cards not found elsewhere.

GW RATING: ★★★★½

These special packs are great for collectors and anyone who loves cool, limited edition cards. They make the game feel really special.

EVENT — PRE-RELEASE TOURNAMENTS

WHAT HAPPENS: Before a new set is officially released players can join pre-release tournaments to get a sneak peek at the new cards. You get a few packs from the latest set to build a deck and compete.

GW RATING: ★★★★★

Pre-release tournaments are super fun because you use new cards before most people have them. Plus, it's a great way to learn the game and meet other Pokémon fans!

EVENT — LEAGUE PLAY

WHAT HAPPENS: Many local game stores have a Pokémon League, where you can play regularly to earn points and badges. It's a casual way to play and perfect for learning the game.

GW RATING: ★★★★☆

League play is awesome for making new friends and improving at the game. It's not as competitive as other events, which makes it more relaxed and fun for everyone.

EVENT — CHAMPIONSHIP SERIES

WHAT HAPPENS: For those who are more competitive, the Pokémon TCG Championship Series is a set of tournaments that lead to national and world championships. You can earn incredible prizes and even scholarships!

GW RATING: ★★★★★

The Championship Series is thrilling and challenging. It's where you can really test your skills and maybe even become a Pokémon Master!

EVENT — SPECIAL EVENTS

WHAT HAPPENS: Throughout the year, there are special events like holiday tournaments or charity events where you can play the TCG in a festive atmosphere.

GW RATING: ★★★★½

Special events are a blast because they mix Pokémon fun with festive celebrations or good causes. They're a great way to enjoy the game and help others at the same time!

GAMESWARRIOR'S VERDICT

We love how the Pokémon Trading Card Game offers something for everyone, whether you're just starting out or ready to take on the world. With new sets and exciting events happening all the time, there's always a new adventure waiting in the world of Pokémon TCG!

LET'S TALK ABOUT

POKÉMON GO

Pokémon GO, the fun game where you can catch Pokémon in the real world, has exciting monthly events that make the game super unique. Let's check out what these events are all about and see why **GamesWarrior** thinks they're so cool.

COMMUNITY DAY

WHAT HAPPENS: This special day happens monthly and lets you find lots of the same Pokémon for a few hours. These Pokémon are everywhere, and you might even find a shiny one! If you evolve this Pokémon during the event, it can learn a special move that it usually can't.

GW RATING: ★★★★★

Community Day is awesome for meeting other trainers and catching lots of Pokémon. The special moves make your Pokémon even stronger for battles!

SPOTLIGHT HOUR

WHAT HAPPENS: Every Tuesday for one hour, a certain Pokémon will pop up more than usual. There are also extra goodies like double XP or more candy when you catch Pokémon.

GW RATING: ★★★★☆

Spotlight Hour is quick and fun! It's a great time to fill up your Pokédex and get lots of candy to help your Pokémon grow.

RAID HOUR

WHAT HAPPENS: On Wednesdays for one hour, there are more raid battles, often including legendary Pokémon. It's a time to join with friends and try to catch some of the strongest Pokémon.

GW RATING: ★★★★½

Raid Hour is super thrilling with many epic battles. Working together with friends to win is the best part!

GO BATTLE LEAGUE SEASONS

WHAT HAPPENS: The Battle League lets you fight against other players in special seasons. You can earn cool rewards based on how well you do.

GW RATING: ★★★★☆

The Battle League is great for showing off your Pokémon skills, and you can get awesome prizes. It might be tough for beginners, but it's really rewarding!

RESEARCH BREAKTHROUGHS

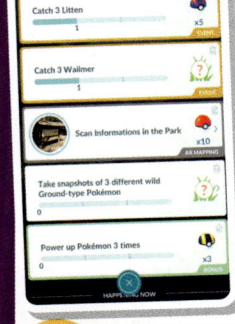

WHAT HAPPENS: If you finish one research task a day for seven days, you get a special surprise Pokémon that you rarely see.

GW RATING: ★★★★★

Research Breakthroughs are exciting because you never know what rare Pokémon you'll get. It's like a mystery box with a Pokémon inside!

SEASONAL EVENTS

WHAT HAPPENS: These events change with the seasons and bring different Pokémon that fit the time of year and fun challenges.

GW RATING: ★★★★½

Seasonal events make the game feel new all the time. It's like going on a new adventure every few months!

GAMESWARRIOR'S VERDICT: GamesWarrior loves how these events keep Pokémon GO fun and fresh, giving everyone something exciting to look forward to every month!

GAME REVIEW
SCARLET AND VIOLET
HIGHLIGHTS

In Paldea, the region of Pokémon Scarlet and Violet, players embark on an exciting journey featuring not just one but three storylines! This groundbreaking approach allows trainers to tackle the challenges in any sequence, making each playthrough unique and full of surprises. Here are the top five moments from these adventures according to **GamesWarrior**.

5: VICTORY ROAD: THE FINAL GYM BATTLE

In a familiar yet thrilling storyline, Victory Road challenges trainers to conquer gyms and ascend to the Pokémon League. The final gym, where you face the Ice-type expert Grusha, stands out as a test of strategy and skill. Overcoming Grusha earns the last badge and proves you're ready for the Elite Four!

GamesWarrior's Verdict: This climactic battle tests all the skills trainers have honed throughout their journey. It's a classic Pokémon experience reimagined, making it both nostalgic and excitingly fresh.

★★★★★

4: STARFALL STREET - THE SHOWDOWN WITH TEAM STAR

The confrontation with Team Star's leader, Cassiopeia, is pivotal in the Starfall Street storyline. This battle is not just about strength but also about strategy as you dismantle the nefarious plans of Team Star, which has caused chaos across the region.

GamesWarrior's Verdict: It's a dramatic peak in the storyline, packed with action and revelations. The buildup to the encounter adds depth to the narrative, making it a memorable highlight.

★★★★★

Penny: I can't fault you on your battle skills at all. No wonder the bosses fell at your hands.

3: PATH OF LEGENDS - THE QUAKING EARTH TITAN BATTLE

Facing off against the Quaking Earth Titan, either Great Tusk in Scarlet or Iron Treads in Violet, is a formidable and exhilarating challenge. This battle tests your ability to adapt and overcome against one of the most powerful creatures in the region.

GamesWarrior's Verdict: This titan battle is a test of strength and a spectacle. Seeing such mighty Pokémon in action is thrilling, and defeating them feels like a true accomplishment.

GW RATING ★★★★½

2: FIRST ENCOUNTER WITH KORAIDON/MIRAIDON

When you first meet your future partner, Koraidon or Miraidon, it's a magical moment setting the tone for your adventure. This encounter is about gaining a new Pokémon and forming a bond that will define your journey through Paldea.

GamesWarrior's Verdict: This moment is heartwarming and establishes a deep connection between the player and their Pokémon. It's a perfect blend of charm and excitement that only Pokémon games can deliver.

GW RATING ★★★★½

1: THE ACADEMY ACE TOURNAMENT

Competing in the academy tournament offers a chance to showcase your growth as a trainer against your peers, including friends you've made along your journey. It's a celebration of your adventures and the friendships you've forged.

GamesWarrior's Verdict: It's more than just battles; it's a culmination of your school year, mixing competition with storytelling. Each match is a step back through the memories of your journey, making it a nostalgic and fulfilling experience.

GW RATING ★★★★☆

Geeta
May you shine as brightly as the future of Paldea, Glimmora!

GAME GUIDE
TEAL DISK

Pokémon Scarlet and Violet's 'The Teal Mask' DLC is a thrilling adventure in Kitakami! This additional content is packed with mystery, challenges, and unique events, making it an unforgettable part of your Pokémon journey. Here are GamesWarrior's top 5 moments from 'The Teal Mask' DLC, each brimming with excitement and wonder!

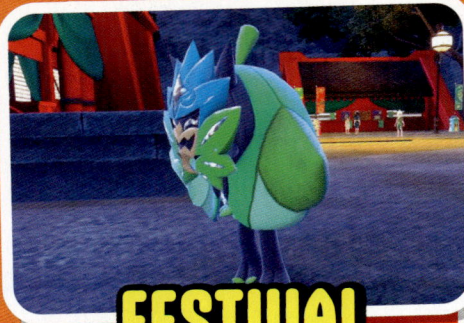

FESTIVAL OF MASKS

Join the vibrant Festival of Masks, where trainers mingle, compete, and celebrate under the guise of beautifully crafted masks. This festival isn't just about fun; it's a deep dive into the local culture and traditions of Kitakami.

GW Rating: ★★★★★

GamesWarrior's Verdict: The festival is a burst of colour and excitement, bringing trainers together in a festive atmosphere. It's a perfect blend of community and competition, making it a standout experience in the DLC.

BATTLE AGAINST THE LOYAL THREE

Face off against the Loyal Three, a trio of unique and powerful Pokémon that guard the secrets of Kitakami. Each battle tests your skills and strategies in new and challenging ways.

GW Rating: ★★★★★

GamesWarrior's Verdict: These encounters are more than just battles; they're epic confrontations that feel like significant milestones in the DLC. Overcoming these guardians is a true testament to a trainer's growth and bravery.

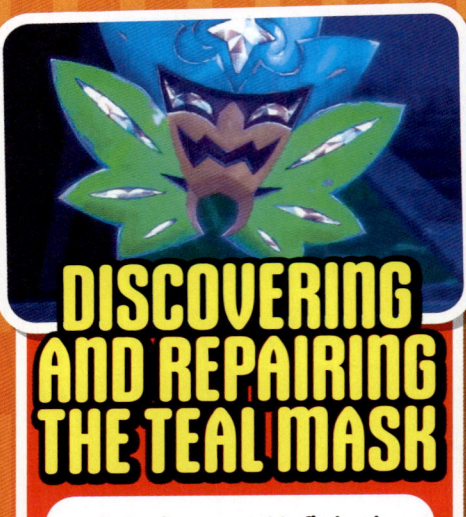

DISCOVERING AND REPAIRING THE TEAL MASK

Embark on a quest to find and restore the mysterious Teal Mask. This journey leads you across Kitakami, unravelling clues and facing challenges that culminate in the restoration of this ancient artefact.

GW Rating: ★★★★½

GamesWarrior's Verdict: The quest blends exploration with puzzle-solving, making it a brain-teasing adventure that rewards ingenuity and persistence. Restoring the Teal Mask feels like making a real difference in the Kitakami world.

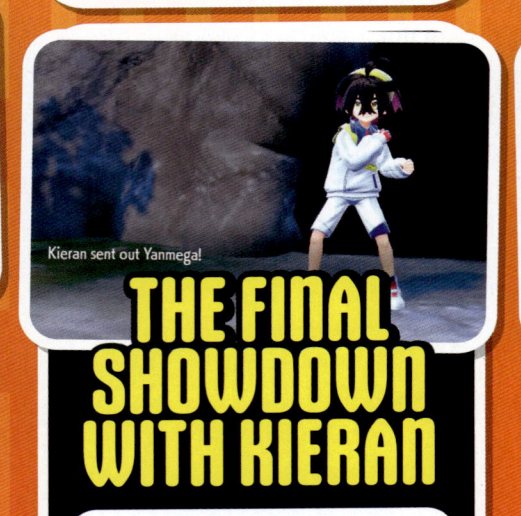

THE FINAL SHOWDOWN WITH KIERAN

Your repeated battles with Kieran throughout the DLC build up to a final, decisive showdown that tests everything you've learned. This climactic battle is about strength and the bonds you've built with your Pokémon.

GW Rating: ★★★★★

GamesWarrior's Verdict: Kieran is a rival who grows with you throughout the DLC, and each encounter adds depth to his character and the overall story. The final battle is emotionally charged and satisfying.

CATCHING OGERPON

After proving your worth through various trials, you get the opportunity to catch Ogerpon, a unique Pokémon linked closely to the Teal Mask. This moment is a rewarding culmination of your adventures in Kitakami.

GW Rating: ★★★★★

GamesWarrior's Verdict: Catching Ogerpon is not just about adding a new Pokémon to your collection; it's about connecting deeply with the lore of Kitakami and becoming a part of its history.

GAME GUIDE
INDIGO DISK

The 'Indigo Disk' DLC in Pokémon Scarlet and Violet brings our young trainers to the prestigious Blueberry Academy as exchange students, opening up a new world of challenges and mysteries. Here are GamesWarrior's top 5 standout moments in the 'Indigo Disk' DLC that you won't want to miss, each packed with excitement and unique experiences!

Cyrano: Look at how blue the place is! I can't tell you how long I spent picking the perfect blueberry color!

JOINING BLUEBERRY ACADEMY

Start your journey by meeting Director Cyrano and becoming an exchange student at Blueberry Academy. This is your gateway to new friendships, battles, and learning!

GW RATING ★★★★★

GamesWarrior's Verdict: It's a fresh start in a new, exciting environment. Being an exchange student adds an interesting twist to your Pokémon adventure, filled with new faces and challenges.

Crispin: Gwah! You're really gonna douse our flames if you keep using moves like that!

THE ELITE FOUR BATTLES

Players challenge the Elite Four of Blueberry Academy, each with unique trials and epic Pokémon battles. These include Crispin's spicy sandwich trial and Amarys' high-flying time trial.

GW RATING ★★★★½

GamesWarrior's Verdict: The trials are fun and test your knowledge and skills in new ways. Each member of the Elite Four brings a distinct flavour to the challenges, making each battle memorable.

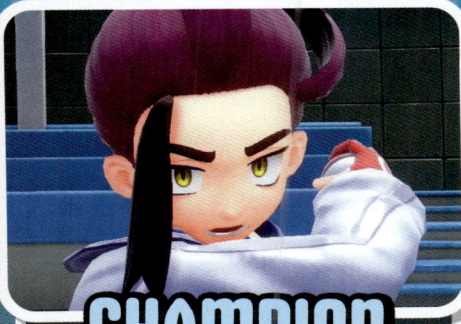

CHAMPION KIERAN SHOWDOWN

Battle against Champion Kieran, the strongest trainer at Blueberry Academy. This ultimate test of skill will push you to your limits!

GW RATING ★★★★½

GamesWarrior's Verdict: Kieran's battle is intense and thrilling, serving as the pinnacle of your journey in the DLC. It's a battle that tests everything you've learned at the Academy.

Briar: OH MY GOODNESS!

AREA ZERO EXPEDITION

Venture into the mysterious Area Zero for a daring expedition. This part of the journey is filled with discoveries and challenges that reveal more about the Pokémon world.

GW RATING ★★★★★

GamesWarrior's Verdict: The expedition is a great mix of exploration and combat, providing insights into the deeper lore of Pokémon. It's an adventure that feels both grand and intriguing.

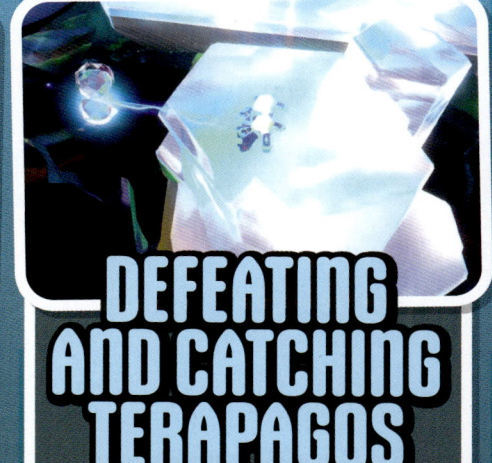

DEFEATING AND CATCHING TERAPAGOS

In an epic conclusion, you must battle and catch Terapagos, the legendary Pokémon of the Indigo Disk. This moment is a major achievement and a dramatic turn in the storyline.

GW RATING ★★★★★

GamesWarrior's Verdict: Catching Terapagos is a rewarding end to a challenging journey. It's a testament to your skills as a Pokémon trainer and provides a satisfying end to the DLC story.

ANIME GUIDE
ASH SAYS GOODBYE

Hey, young trainers! Grab your Pokédex and get ready for some big news from Pokémon. It's time to wave goodbye to our longtime friend, Ash Ketchum, and his faithful companion, Pikachu, as they depart from the Pokémon anime series. After over two decades of adventure, that's more than a thousand episodes, Ash and Pikachu are passing the torch in the newest series, 'Pokémon Horizons'. Here's GamesWarrior's thoughts on this epic adventure.

ASH KETCHUM'S EPIC JOURNEY

Ash has been the heart of the Pokémon anime since the very beginning. Alongside Pikachu, he travelled far and wide, met tons of Pokémon, and faced countless challenges. They've won big battles, made many friends, and even took on the Pokémon League!

Why We Love It: Ash showed us that anyone can become a great Pokémon Trainer with determination and a kind heart. His journey has been inspiring, showing us how to courageously face challenges and always stand up for what's right.

GW Rating: ★★★★★

MEGA EVOLUTIONS

In their final episode, 'Aim To Be A Pokemon Master', Ash and Pikachu encountered some old friends and rivals. They even bumped into their old troublemaking adversaries, Team Rocket, and Ash reunited with his Pidgeot, a Pokémon he hadn't seen in years! There were tears and smiles as Ash said a heartfelt goodbye to his friends Misty and Brock, reminding us all about the strong bonds of friendship.

Why We Love It: This episode was a rollercoaster of emotions and surprises, perfectly wrapping up Ash's journey while reminding us of all the incredible adventures we've shared.

GW Rating: ★★★★½

WHAT'S NEXT FOR ASH AND PIKACHU?

As Ash and Pikachu walked down a new path, Ash shared some wise word with us — becoming a Pokémon Master is a never-ending journey. It's about growing, learning, and enjoying the adventure, no matter where it takes you.

Why We Love It: Ash's parting words left us thinking about our journeys. His story might be pausing for now, but the spirit of adventure and exploration in Pokémon continues.

GW Rating: ★★★★☆

WILL ASH RETURN?

There's a little hint from the show's director, Kunihiko Yuyama, that Ash and Pikachu might return someday. Now, with Ash having reached his dream of becoming a Pokémon world champion, who knows? Maybe we'll see him return as a Pokémon Master!

Why We Love It: The door is open for more stories, and the thought of Ash and Pikachu returning someday keeps the excitement alive.

GW Rating: ★★★★☆

ANIME GUIDE
ASH'S LAST MOVIE?

Could Ash Ketchum and Pikachu return in a brand new Pokémon movie set after 'Secrets of the Jungle'? It would be an incredible opportunity for fans to see their favorite duo back in action. Let's explore what we can expect from this movie and why it's significant for Pokémon enthusiasts.

ASH'S POSSIBLE RETURN: WHAT'S THE BUZZ?
Ash and Pikachu have been the beloved stars of Pokémon for more than 20 years. Though on a break, the director of the anime hinted at their grand comeback. If Ash returns, he'll still be the same 10-year-old adventurer we all love.

GW RATING: ★★★★½

Why We Love It: Ash's youthful spirit of adventure will never fade, inspiring new generations of fans.

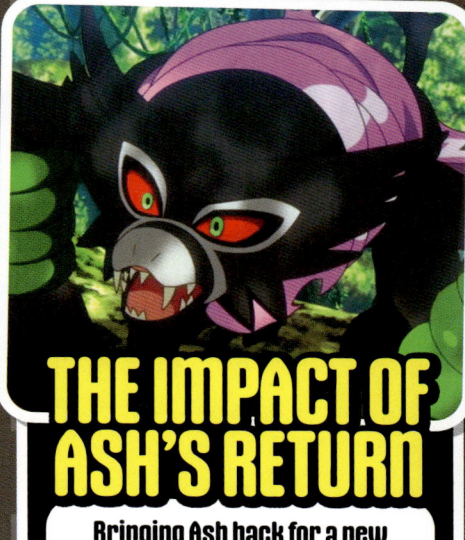

THE IMPACT OF ASH'S RETURN
Bringing Ash back for a new Pokémon movie would connect his past adventures to new challenges in the Pokémon universe. Other original series characters might appear, bridging old with new and keeping the nostalgia alive.

GW RATING: ★★★★½

Why We Love It: It gives fans old and new something to be excited about.

BEING CAREFUL WITH ASH'S RETURN
Ash and Pikachu's return to 'Pokemon Horizons' is thrilling, but the new characters, Liko and Roy, should not be overshadowed. They need their own time to shine without being outshone by Ash.

GW RATING: ★★★½☆

Why It's Tricky: It's all about timing and making sure everyone gets their moment in the spotlight.

WHY ASH'S RETURN COULD BE A BIG HIT
Ash's return could be a major event for Pokémon. It would celebrate its history and future. Ash could guide or join new heroes.

GW RATING: ★★★★★

Why We Love It: It would blend old and new adventures, making it a celebration of everything that makes Pokémon great.

THE FUTURE WITH ASH?
Pokémon fans eagerly await Ash and Pikachu's return. Their comeback, whether a surprise appearance or a new movie, would be a highlight for all.

GW RATING: ★★★★★

Why We Love It: We'll keep our Pokéballs ready for the next Pokémon adventure.

ANIME GUIDE
POKÉMON HORIZONS

Welcome to a new adventure with 'Pokémon Horizons', where the world of Pokémon is bigger and bolder than ever before! Since Ash's departure, the Pokémon anime has taken a fresh turn, introducing new heroes like Liko and Roy, who are ready to capture your hearts. Check out GamesWarrior's top 5 moments from 'Pokémon Horizons' so far, and see why each one is so special.

FIRST POKEMON BATTLE

'Pokémon Horizons' kicks off with Liko's first ever Pokémon battle, where she teams up with her new partner, Sprigatito. It's not just any fight; it's a moment of courage as Liko steps out of her comfort zone, showing that she's ready to face whatever comes her way.

GW RATING: ★★★★★

Why We Love It: This moment sets the stage for Liko's journey, mixing excitement with the thrill of the unknown. It's a fantastic start that promises lots of adventure.

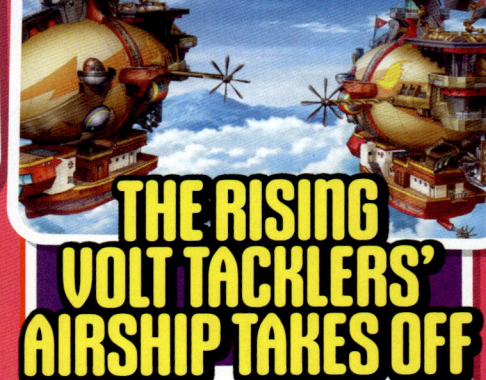

THE RISING VOLT TACKLERS' AIRSHIP TAKES OFF

Imagine an airship soaring through the skies, carrying Liko and a band of quirky characters like Mollie and Orla. This isn't just transport; it's a symbol of the vast world of Pokémon waiting to be explored.

GW RATING: ★★★★½

Why We Love It: This scene is a blast of fresh air, literally taking the series to new heights and showing that 'Horizons' is all about grand adventures.

AMETHIO'S THREAT

When the menacing Amethio confronts Liko, demanding her grandmother's mysterious pendant, it's not just a battle — it's a test of Liko's resolve. The intensity and stakes introduce a darker, more thrilling layer to the Pokémon world.

GW RATING: ★★★★½

Why It's Tricky: This moment adds depth to the story, weaving mystery and danger into Liko's journey, making every episode a gripping watch.

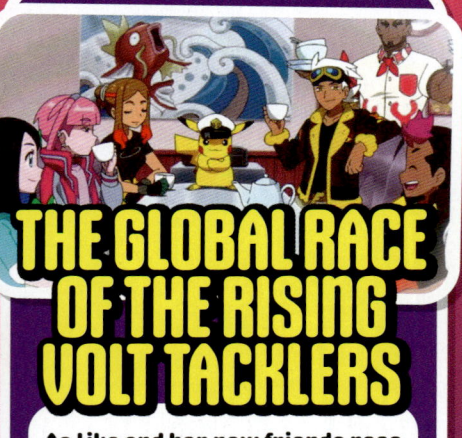

THE GLOBAL RACE OF THE RISING VOLT TACKLERS

As Liko and her new friends race across different regions, the series takes on an adventurous, almost 'One Piece-like' quality. This global trek connects the Pokémon world in ways we've never seen before in the anime.

GW RATING: ★★★★½

Why We Love It: It's thrilling to see how interconnected the Pokémon world is, and each new location brings its own set of challenges and wonders, keeping us glued to our screens.

LIKO AND SPRIGATITO'S GROWING BOND

Throughout their challenges, the bond between Liko and her Pokémon strengthens, mirroring her personal growth. Their relationship is a heartwarming reminder of the core of Pokémon: friendship and growth through adventure.

GW RATING: ★★★★★

Why We Love It: This ongoing development is a beautiful portrayal of teamwork and perseverance, showing us that Liko is becoming a true Pokémon trainer, one battle at a time.

ANIME GUIDE
MUST WATCH SERIES

If Pokémon Trainers have been exploring the vast regions of Pokémon Scarlet and Violet, they'll want to check out the anime series Paldean Winds and Pokémon Concierge. Here's why these series are must-sees for every Pokémon fan, according to GamesWarrior.

PALDEAN WINDS: DISCOVERING PALDEA

Ever felt like the beauty of the Paldea region in Pokémon Scarlet and Violet didn't fully shine through? Paldean Winds is here to show you the true splendour of Paldea, free from any game bugs or graphical limitations. This four-part anime mini-series takes you on a stunning visual journey, showcasing the lush landscapes and iconic locations of Paldea in breathtaking detail.

Why we love it Each episode of Paldean Winds is like a bit of treasure, giving us a deeper appreciation of the game's world. The animation quality is so high that you'll feel like you're seeing Paldea for the first time, making it essential viewing for any fan of the Pokémon Scarlet and Violet games. The final episode, especially with its group project showcasing Paldea's highlights, is a visual treat that redefines our connection to the game.

GW RATING ★★★★★

POKÉMON CONCIERGE: A RELAXING RETREAT WITH YOUR FAVOURITE POKEMON

Switch gears with Pokémon Concierge, a unique stop-motion series that offers a soothing, slice-of-life experience. Join Haru, the newest employee at the Pokémon Resort, as she learns to unwind and help Pokémon guests with their little worries. It's a world away from battles and adventures, focusing instead on relaxation and the emotional journeys of Pokémon and humans.

Why we love it Pokémon Concierge is a breath of fresh air in the Pokémon universe. Its gorgeous stop-motion animation brings Pokémon to life in an adorable and incredibly real way. The series is a perfect blend of cosy and comforting, making it a great choice for anyone looking to take a break from the usual high-energy Pokémon battles. The show's emphasis on mental health and self-care adds a meaningful layer that resonates with viewers of all ages.

GW RATING ★★★★☆

ANIME GUIDE
WHAT'S NEXT?

POKÉMON LIVE-ACTION SERIES ON NETFLIX

Pokémon is set to come alive in a brand-new way! Netflix is developing a live-action Pokémon series that promises to bring the beloved world of Pokémon into the real world, much like what we saw in Detective Pikachu. With the prospect of some exciting storytelling, it could explore new areas or revisit classic Pokémon adventures.

Why It's Worth the Watch: For Pokémon fans, young and old, this series is poised to offer a fresh take on the Pokémon universe. Whether it follows the familiar journey of Ash or introduces new characters and stories, the live-action format will bring Pokémon to life in unprecedented ways. Given Netflix's track record with series, there's a good chance they'll do justice to the Pokémon world. Plus, it's a great way to introduce the magic of Pokémon to newcomers.

GW Rating: ★★★★★

If you've been wondering what's next in the Pokémon universe, there's some exciting news you won't want to miss. **GamesWarrior** gets into why you should keep your eyes peeled for the upcoming Pokémon live-action Netflix series and the possibility of a new Detective Pikachu movie.

DETECTIVE PIKACHU 2

Following the success of the first Detective Pikachu movie, a sequel is in the works. However, its development has seen some delays. The first movie offered a unique look at the Pokémon world, blending humour, mystery, and the thrill of Pokémon battles in a live-action and CGI setting. While the exact details of the sequel's story are still under wraps, the continuation will likely delve deeper into the Pokémon universe with new adventures and maybe even some new characters.

Why You Should Be Excited: The first Detective Pikachu movie was a hit, providing a mix of nostalgia for long-time fans and a fun introduction for those new to Pokémon. A sequel could expand on this universe, exploring more complex plots and maybe even introducing us to other regions or Pokémon not seen in the first film. The blend of live-action and CGI in Detective Pikachu set a high bar for visual effects, offering a unique way to experience the charm of Pokémon.

GW RATING: ★★★★☆

CONSOLE REVIEW
HISTORY OF

Nintendo and Pokémon have a long history filled with fun and adventures that many kids and adults love! Here's a short breakdown of Nintendo consoles and the exciting Pokémon games that came with them. Each console also has a special **GamesWarrior** verdict explaining why it's so cool!

POKÉMON GAMES:
POKÉMON RED
POKÉMON BLUE
POKÉMON YELLOW

POKÉMON GAMES:
POKÉMON STADIUM
POKÉMON SNAP

POKÉMON GAMES:
POKÉMON RUBY AND SAPPHIRE
POKÉMON FIRERED
LEAFGREEN

1996
GAME BOY

The first handheld Pokémon Adventures launched in Japan with Pokémon Red and Green. This was followed in 1998 with the worldwide launch of Pokémon Red and Blue.

GW RATING ★★★★★

The Game Boy is super special because it's where Pokémon first began! The first portable device made it possible for kids everywhere to catch and train Pokémon anywhere they went.

1996
NINTENDO 64

The Nintendo 64 brought Pokémon into the living room with bigger, bolder graphics.

GW RATING ★★★★☆

Pokémon Stadium let everyone see their Pokémon battle in 3D!

2001
GAME BOY ADVANCE

With brighter colours and more Pokémon, the well designed Game Boy Advance made exploring new regions lots of fun.

GW RATING ★★★★½

The Game Boy Advance made catching Pokémon even more exciting.

NINTENDO AND POKÉMON

POKÉMON GAMES
POKÉMON DIAMOND AND PEARL
POKÉMON BLACK AND WHITE

POKÉMON GAMES:
POKÉMON X
Y, POKÉMON SUN AND MOON

POKÉMON GAMES
POKÉMON SWORD AND SHIELD
LEGENDS ARCEUS
POKÉMON LET'S GO PIKACHU AND EEVEE
POKÉMON SCARLET AND VIOLET

2004
NINTENDO DS

With two screens and wireless connectivity, the Nintendo DS was a game-changer.

GW RATING ★★★★½

Battling and navigating the Pokémon world became doubly fun!

2011
NINTENDO 3DS

With awesome 3D graphics and online connection, players had the ability to chat with friends far away.

GW RATING ★★★★★

With its cool features the Nintendo 3DS took Pokémon adventures with friends to the next level.

2017
NINTENDO SWITCH

With removable controllers, the Nintendo Switch mixed things up by letting you play at home and on the go.

GW RATING ★★★★★

Throwing Pokéballs with a flick of the Switch controller, Pokémon battles are cooler than ever!

LET'S EXPLORE POKÉMON REGIONS

Exploring different regions is a big part of what makes Pokémon games so much fun! Each region is unique, with its own special Pokémon and exciting adventures. Here are **GamesWarrior**'s top 5 Pokémon regions and why we think each one is super cool!

GAMESWARRIOR'S TOP 5 POKÉMON REGIONS

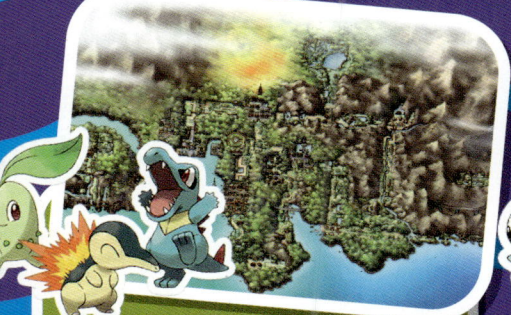

5 JOHTO REGION

Johto is where tradition meets mystery! This region has ancient lore and beautiful cities that feel like you're stepping back in time. There are places like the Bell Tower and the Ruins of Alph to explore, plus the chance to visit Kanto.

GW RATING: ★★★★★

Johto offers a magical adventure rich in history and fun!

4 SINNOH REGION

Sinnoh is a region that balances nature with big industries and where you can challenge the mighty Mt. Coronet. Full of folklore and legendary stories, every trip feels like a new discovery in Sinnoh!

GW RATING: ★★★★½

If you like snowy mountains and myths about legendary Pokémon, Sinnoh is your place!

3 ALOLA REGION

Inspired by Hawaii, this region is a tropical paradise. Alola swaps traditional Gym battles for Island Trials, which are fun challenges that teach respect for nature. Plus, those beautiful beaches make every day a vacation!

GW RATING: ★★★★½

Say aloha to Alola, where the sun always shines, and the adventures never end!

2 HOENN REGION

Hoenn is perfect for trainers who love exploring and experiencing the wild side of the Pokémon world. With its vast ocean and dramatic weather changes, you can dive underwater or help stop massive weather catastrophes.

GW RATING: ★★★★☆

With secret bases to build and decorate, Hoenn is an adventurer's dream!

1 GALAR REGION

Inspired by the UK, Galar is known for its charming countryside and modern cities. It introduces exciting Dynamax battles, where Pokémon turn giant! The region is innovative and full of energy, hosting the Champion Cup instead of traditional Pokémon League battles.

GW RATING: ★★★★☆

This dynamic region makes every competition feel like a grand event!

GAMESWARRIOR'S VERDICT

Each of these regions brings something special to the world of Pokémon. Whether you're exploring ancient ruins, diving deep into the ocean, or battling gigantic Pokémon in grand stadiums, there's a perfect spot for every young trainer to start their adventure!